RETAIL

REDEMPTION

AT

$8.25

AN HOUR

MIKE FREEDMAN

 FriesenPress

One Printers Way
Altona, MB R0G 0B0
Canada

www.friesenpress.com

ISBN
978-1-03-910412-9 (Hardcover)
978-1-03-910411-2 (Paperback)
978-1-03-910413-6 (eBook)

1. *FICTION, COMING OF AGE*

Distributed to the trade by The Ingram Book Company

CONTENTS

Prologue. 1

Beyond Here Lies Nothin'. 11

Born In Time. 13

Don't Think Twice, It's alright. 17

Down The Highway. 23

Everything Is Broken. 25

Every Grain of Sand. 29

God Knows. 33

Gotta Serve Somebody. 35

Hero Blues. 43

Hurricane. 47

I Feel a Change Comin' On. 49

If You Belonged. 53

Idiot Wind. 57

My Back Pages. 63

Someone's Got a Hold of My Heart. 67

Turkey Chase. 71

Winterlude. 73

Simple Twist of Fate. 77

Shake Shake Mama. 81

On A Night Like This. 85

New Blue Moon. 87

Never Gonna Be the Same Again. 89

Neighborhood Bully. 91

Let's Keep It Between Us. 95

Baby, I'm In the Mood for You 97

7 Deadly Sins. 99

Day Of the Locusts. 103

Dirt Road Blues 105

Love Minus Zero/No Limit. 107

Maybe Someday 109

Nothing Was Delivered 113

Odds And Ends 115

Only A Pawn in Their Game. 117

Pledging My Time 119

Ring Them Bells 123

Round And Round We Go 129

Tell Me That It Isn't True 131

Tragedy Of the Trade. 133

You Own a Racehorse 137

Summer Days 145

Spirit On the Water 149

Sitting On a Barbed Wire Fence. 151

Series Of Dreams 153

Romance In Durango 159

Pressing On. 163

Political World 169

Pay In Blood 173

Epilogue. 177

The Years After! 179

Prologue

All-American Boy

1994 was a great year for music if you were in or near LA, New York, or Seattle. To bear witness to the defining music of an entire generation was a unique and rare privilege, yet to be trapped in the Midwest, in Grafton, far from the epicentre, was torturous.

It's not a matter of conjecture that some of the most important music of all time, certainly since the mid-seventies, was released in the early nineties. The sixties and its lofty but beautiful idealism grew into the arena rock and new age revolution of the seventies. By the eighties, music had hit a wall. Style become more important than substance and by 1990, modern music appeared doomed and in decline. Then along came Cobain, and everything changed for about four wonderful years.

1994 was the musical high-water mark for several convergent generations as Gen X passed the baton of youth to Gen Y and the last of the hippies accepted their middle age. After 1994 there was still good music but that was it. *That* moment had peaked and then faded. As the nineties gave way to the next millennium the dream had all but died. It started as Nirvana and ended with Nickleback.

Hunter was one of the people watching history from the outside looking in, 18 and nearing the end of school. The son of the local doctor, he grew up in the small town of Grafton, North Dakota. Along with a few other lucky kids (whose parents owned the 3 stores, 2 car dealerships, the grocery store, gas station and mill) Hunter had a way out of the prison of Grafton and not just to Fargo, Grand Forks or even Minneapolis.

He had no problem with ND, he just sought more from life than he could ever get there. He sensed that the defining music of his generation was playing out and he was missing it, he had an overwhelming need to get out. He was blessed with real options to escape but lacked the discipline to exercise any of them. His father was right: he just didn't take life seriously enough.

His father was disappointed in nearly all he had done. He was equally disappointed in all he had not done. Hunter was smart enough to get into any number of good schools in North Dakota (not on a full scholarship mind you) but his grades were ok enough. He had no sense of ambition. Everything he had: the car, the stereo, the clothes… all from dad. He drank too much at parties. He smoked a little dope on weekends. He prioritized having fun over working hard… at least according to the consensus of his parents, numerous relatives, his friends' parents, his teachers, his past coaches and even their pastor.

His father had a very clear arrangement with him and had been up front about it since he was 14: maintain a simple B+ average and his education would be well and fully funded. He would want for nothing and would receive a credit card in addition to having his tuition and housing costs covered. However, Hunter had a C+ average and knew, under no uncertain terms, that not only would school not be funded but that he would also need to leave home.

There were government loans and assistance grants, but he knew that he would not qualify for any of them. One look at the car he drove up in and he knew he would be shown the door. They asked for the income of your parents if you still lived at home… they were not going to give a loan to a kid whose dad was a wealthy doctor.

There were very few options in a Grafton and while he knew his friend's father would give him a job at the mill, even a good job at the local mill was a fate worse than death. Some of his friends had no other choice. The working life was to be their lives as it was their parents' lives (and in many cases, their grandparents' lives) too. Once from Grafton, forever from Grafton.

There were not a lot of places to unwind in Grafton on a Tuesday night in mid-June, after a day of bad news. He contemplated a life filled with punch cards, 3 weeks of vacation a year and monthly payments on cars, apartments and pretty much everything else. Consumed by his lack of future, he needed to find something to do where the beer was also sufficiently cold. There was only one option: he made his way to the local bowling alley – Small's Balls – and with a few friends, decided to have a few games and bowl a few frames.

Smalls didn't care how old you were, as long as you had cash in hand you could get a beer.

Drinks were ordered, ugly shoes were laced tight. Iridescent bowling balls were chosen, flecks of glitter embedded in the green, red, amber and blue spheres. An unplanned game in lane 7 was about to change everything though.

Hunter wasn't traditionally a great bowler; indeed, he had been just okay the few times he had bowled years ago at birthday parties or school trips. The legal age was 21 but in small towns it was more of a guideline than a rule and Small's wasn't the only place in town to get a drink so by the time he got there he had already enjoyed a number of drinks.

Usually, after bad news, drinking until you didn't care was a normal but frowned upon thing, but that night it would work in Hunter's favor. His friends took their turns and then it was his turn. Hunter stepped up to the line and threw his bright red ball as hard as he could.

He was thinking of his father as he was throwing. He thought of his teachers who told him he would never accomplish as much as his father. He thought of waiting in a line to punch in for his morning shift.

Facing a radical departure from his hopes and dreams while only taking moderate responsibility for his own inaction, he felt dismayed and angry as he threw the ball towards the pins.

He wasn't thinking, he simply aimed at the pins and let loose. The ball hit the pins with equal parts ferocity and velocity, every one of them went flying. It was a strike! He laughed it off as beginner's luck and went back to sulking about his future.

His friends played their turns: spares and a few close calls but Hunter was on the board with the high score. When his second turn came his throw was propelled by the same powerful emotions welling below the surface, a young man staring into the abyss of mediocrity. Another massive strike!

Frame by frame, he was consistent. Pins were flying and people were watching. It's not that a near perfect game was unique to the fine sport of bowling, but it was fairly rare in Small's Balls. People there bowled for the love of bowling and Grafton had not produced any bowlers of note.

As the game ended Hunter had done what few others have or will do, he had accidentally played a perfect game! One person, in particular, was watching the young (but rather boisterous and slightly inebriated) man closely. At the time, nobody knew the significance of the red T-Shirt the man was wearing with a U of W logo on it.

A second game began and while not perfect (he missed 3 pins on a frame because he claimed to have slipped) it was clear that he was one of the best players to ever grace Small's Balls. He had the best score anyone could remember and by game 3 pretty much everyone had stopped to watch him throw.

Remember when we heard Nevermind, BloodSugarSexMagic or 10 for the first time? Remember how it felt, hearing something and just knowing that it was profound and was going to change the world? Now imagine that feeling but with bowling. To those people there that night, seeing the kid bowl was like that first time we pressed play and turned up the volume!

Hunter didn't really care though; he didn't even recognize what he had just done and was still doing. Even a good game of bowling couldn't erase the feeling of starting to realize that the moment he was living in right then was probably the best it was going to get. That was until the man in the red U of W t-shirt walked over to introduce himself.

His name was Roger Beebock, and he was the assistant coach of the bowling team at University of Winnipeg. While bowling is not as popular of a university sport as football, track, volleyball, hockey or basketball, it was nonetheless a very passionately followed sport. When it came to university level bowling, U of W was not one of the big schools, it was *THE* school. They were always seeking an edge to maintain their dominance of the college bowling scene (6 titles in the last 20 years thank you very much! Go Pins!!). There in Small's Balls, Roger Beebock was convinced that he had found a way for U of W to do just that.

Hunter listened and laughed, he thought someone was playing a joke on him, so he didn't take it seriously. Then Roger asked him which school he signed with and how his grades were. None but pretty good was the answer and that was when life changed forever.

Roger gave him his card and asked Hunter to call him on Friday morning. One of the advantages of coaching or playing for a top ranked bowling school is that alumni are generous and scholarships are plentiful for the right caliber of player. Hunter was the right caliber of player; he simply needed to get good grades and show up to bowling practice 3 nights a week and to all of the tournaments during the season. Everything would be covered – all he had to do was do something he was already naturally gifted at.

Winnipeg, while only 2 ½ hours from Grafton, was literally in another country. Hunter had his doubts about going to school in Canada but he also knew that it may have been his only shot at escaping Grafton.

Winnipeg is a gritty prairie city, often referred to as the gateway to the west. It was hot in summer and cold in winter but inhabited by some of the most friendly and warm people in the world. After spending a night at the Delta downtown as a guest of U of W, Hunter toured the campus and met with the bowling faculty.

Roger was an amazing salesman and Hunter left the campus with 3 things. The first was the jacket they presented to him, his own U of W jacket with a bowling team crest. The second was a severe dislike of his new head coach who didn't appear to like him that much at all and who talked down to him throughout the entirety of their brief conversation. Lastly, he had a move in date of August 28th and would begin his time as a student at U of W shortly thereafter.

***

As far as school went, Hunter did ok and kept a decent average. Despite wishing he didn't have to attend practice so often, he did even better on the lanes. He was curious as to why the coach used a whistle at a bowling alley and why he yelled so much but like many great coaches, you couldn't argue with the results.

By October the legendary bowling coach, Ron Neufeld, had started to expend a lot more energy and time on Hunter than all of the other bowlers combined. Hunter just assumed that coach hated him. He got yelled at, singled out and often made to stay late at practice. When everyone else would go, coach would keep him late, push him harder. There were frequent reminders of how hard coach had to work in life to get there and how easy Hunter had it. According to coach, Hunter not only didn't have to work hard… he didn't even appreciate the talents and gifts he had.

Hunter's father had been impressed that his son had gotten a scholarship of any sort. Having spent the last 4 years hoping for the best and expecting the worst, some success was a welcome change. He didn't get a credit card and he didn't get everything paid for but he was allowed to keep his car so he could make the drive back and forth from Winnipeg.

After a string of massive tournament wins in the fall of 1994, U of W was again ranked the number 1 seeded school and Hunter was their number 1 player. Hunter took them all the way to bowling's version of the final 4 where they finished 1st. Hunter was even featured on the cover of Sports Illustrated as one of 20 college athletes to watch.

April of 1994 was a bad month all around. It began with the stress of exams and the impending sadness of knowing "that" year and "that" moment in time would soon be coming to an end. On April 5th Hunter's generation lost their unwilling leader when Kurt Cobain took his talent and his life to the grave… though the world would have to wait 3 days to realize their loss.

It wasn't just Darryl Strawberry or Richard Nixon who were having a rough April, Hunter also had a very bad month. Towards the end of April, he met a local girl at a party to celebrate the end of exams. Under the pretext of listening to some music on his car stereo, he was able to get her to leave the party and come back to quad near the residences. At the end of the night, hanging out in his illegally parked car and trying to seal the deal, Hunter began his fall from grace. The school's star athlete drove a car most people knew and he had parked it in a faculty spot, earning the attention of campus police.

When they came upon his black Monte Carlo, they found the windows fogged up and 2 students in what the senior officer described as an open mouth hug! Simply wanting to make sure that both parties were on the same page and consenting (they were), they were asked to step out of the vehicle.

As their ID's were presented, Hunter was pretty sure that he would be ok. As a star athlete and having done nothing illegal or wrong, he assumed he was going to be asked to move along. However, the reaction of the officers when they looked at the girl's ID was enough for him to him to be concerned. The senior officer told them both to hold on as he pulled out his bulky cellular phone and had a hushed call a few feet away.

15 minutes later, Coach Neufeld arrived, angrily exited his Yukon. Expecting to get yelled at just like he had been all year, he was surprised when coach brushed past him and started to yell at the girl instead. Even more surprising was why. When Hunter realized what was going on he began to sweat profusely. This was going to be much worse than anything the police might have done to him... she was his coaches 17-year-old (but much older looking) daughter!

Coach Neufeld didn't yell at him at all, in fact after quickly glaring at Hunter, he said nothing. He grabbed his daughter, got into his Yukon and drove into the night. The older officer told Hunter that he was free to go but that coach was really, really, really, really, extremely, really, really mad.

The next morning, while he was still asleep, the phone in his dorm room rang. It was Roger and in a defeated voice, asked him to come to the office for 11am sharp. He met Hunter at the front door of the faculty office to explain that Coach was really, really, really angry and felt very disappointed in his daughter and his star player for bringing negative attention to them. Hunter tried to explain that he didn't know (he truly didn't) who she was or her age! Roger interjected that was the only reason he was not getting kicked out of school outright.

Hunter felt relieved and walked into the office expecting to get yelled at, maybe punished in some way but assuming life would go on as it had before. Life would go on but not in any way he could have ever predicted.

Hunter sat down with Roger in a chair across from the coach's desk at 10:58 and waited his 11am sharp arrival in his office. Not unlike clockwork, he walked into the office and began to discuss the situation while showing surprising restraint. He explained that he lost a lot of sleep the previous night trying to figure out how to best deal with Hunter.

He knew Hunter was talented and not a bad human being, but he was young, arrogant and unfocussed. He needed to grow up. A lot! He needed to stop being the spoiled athlete and the wealthy doctor's son! So as the coach explained, he would deal with his problem by giving Hunter some time off to smarten up and pull himself together.

He calmly explained that there are several loopholes in the constitution of U of W. One was a loophole relating to a rarely enforced 10pm curfew on campus during exams. Citing the breach of curfew, Hunter would be suspended for a full year. He would not be allowed to maintain an affiliation to his team or NCAA bowling for 1 year. He would lose his scholarship funding for the following year and would have to leave the main campus immediately after exams.

The only thing he was going to get was a roof over his head. His scholarship had included housing for 4 years at U of W and as part of the housing and meal plan, he had to sign a lease document for 4 full years. The lease was for year-round accommodation, but he could be assigned to any dormitory at the discretion of the school. Winnipeg had several laws to protect tenants in regard to breaking a lease so they couldn't kick him out. Doing so would have left the school open to legal action so he wasn't going to be homeless, but he would be responsible for rent starting in September through the following September (his first year was already paid in full).

They couldn't get around the lease itself but there was an option to do the next best thing! The school maintained a small southern campus on the other side of town, 45 minutes away, a remnant from the baby boomers and soldiers returning from wars fought decades before. It was a working-class area where all of the factories were. The houses were all built during WW2 and all were small and run down.

The dorms there were practically empty and though they were occasionally rented out to students from other schools who visited for athletic events, they were otherwise empty, unused, severely neglected and falling into disrepair.

Coach sneered when he explained that it would actually be illegal to kick him out onto the street due to the signed lease, but the law didn't specify where they had to house him on campus. They couldn't kick him out, but they could exile him to the "colonies" and ban him from the main campus!

He was to get a suite in Huron Hall. Huron Hall was an old Holiday Inn which was condemned by the city in 1979. The school bought it for a dollar and many of the students who were housed there felt that same dollar was the last dollar the school ever spent on the building.

It was not luxury living. He was to get a dilapidated former hotel room while in exile. He got a small counter with a hotplate as his kitchen and a bathroom sink which was also his kitchen sink. No roommates or neighbors aside from the old eastern European couple who lived there and also worked as the caretakers. He was not allowed on the main campus or at any official school events. He may have remained in Winnipeg but for all intents and purposes, he was marooned on a desert island.

After exams finished he knew he couldn't go back to Grafton. His family and his friends… he couldn't bear to face them. So, he decided to stay in Winnipeg and find a job; Canada wasn't so bad.

He had a year to ride out and needed to eat, drink and pay the bills. He also knew that he would need to reapply to school if the coach let him back on the team and would need to show something for his year.

In a period of weeks, he had gone from being top ranked college bowler, on the cover of Sports Illustrated to an outcast, unemployed, barred from school and too ashamed to go home.

Beyond Here Lies Nothin'

The night before he began his job search, Hunter sat in his 100% non-air-conditioned suite, watching his 19" TV and trying to find something to watch on the 4 or so channels that regularly came in clearly. The university was not about to invest in cable or A/C for the lone exile in Huron Hall.

The next morning, all he wanted to do was play some music in his car and drive around in the glorious A/C. But, even if he could afford gas to run his car all day, he knew that driving around that side of town and looking for work in his car would not be a good idea. Nobody would give a kid with a car like that a job without asking too many questions; he decided to walk

He had created a stack of resumes and tried to make them look as good as possible. Work experience, no. Life experience, yes (actually no but at 19 he knew everything). Skills: bowling. He hit the road and applied to any place where there was a door!

He applied at a lighting store where he was interviewed by an angry, bug-eyed lady yelling at her staff periodically while saying it was a great place to work and everyone was family… then more yelling.

He applied at a gas station where he met 2 guys with long receding hair. They looked like burnouts who sniffed way too much gas… the older guy explained that they hung out, listened to tunes, enjoyed a few fumes and filled a few tanks… no thanks!

He tried to apply to a bowling alley but was told by the owner that "this is a bowling town: we are all U of W Pins here and if you hurt one of us, you hurt all of us!"

Hunter asked if their opinion would change if he didn't know she was the coach's daughter? His words didn't matter, the local bowling community was united in their shunning of their former star bowler!

Bars and restaurants were the worst to apply to.

Every time he asked to speak to the manager he was intercepted by a gatekeeper who attempted to head him off and take his resume for future consideration.

Other people, when pressed, assured him that they would find the manager and return with someone else, who in turn, assured him that he or she would pass along his resume to the real manager… unless he liked to fight, then they were always hiring bouncers.

Factories were looking for a long-term commitment, a year or less and it wasn't even worth their time to train someone. The money was great but the work was hard and repetitive.

Looking for work is a disheartening prospect if you are not a 'something'. A doctor, plumber, accountant, teacher, trucker or lawyer may change jobs, but they rarely look for work. Those people who were not a 'something' take what they can get and if they cannot get anything, it's even harder.

After 3 days of rejection, terrible offers, crazy people and flat-out no's, Hunter began to walk back to his suite. With 1 remaining resume in his hand, and with nothing remaining to lose, he walked past the big red Retail Depot and stopped. On a whim, he turned around and walked across the parking lot and through those automatic doors.

Born In Time

Each Retail Depot was a massive building with one soul and one sole purpose: to wrangle every cent possible from each and every consumer who walked through those automated sliding glass doors!

There were bright red metal shelves that seemed to reach to the skies above.

The first 8 vertical feet were products the consumer could grab themselves; the next 12 vertical feet were larger items. These were master containers of product, big items, skids of product and back seats belonging to mini vans owned by various staff members. There were also a lot of discontinued products and even a well-hidden apartment: one of the world's first tiny homes.

Each 8-foot horizontal section was 1 big sales pitch. As an example, if you needed some 12 x 12 tiles for the bathroom: there were tiles, all of the stuff you needed to lay them, cutting and measuring tools, knee pads, safety goggles, motivational posters to help you lay tile better, special tile laying hats, tile prayer scrolls and about 43 other things you <u>might</u> need.

You thought you were going in to buy 25 tiles worth $2 each, about $50, right?

Wrong!

You leave with $300 worth of stuff that you can return if you need to but probably won't remember to.

Upon entering the store, Hunter was confronted by a colossal space filled with red monoliths to consumerism. A seemingly endless shrine to everything a human could ever want or need for their home or office. People, forklifts and various types of carts all moved about in a cacophony of organized confusion! Every single being was on a mission to sell, get or put away something.

As he walked to the front of the store, Hunter was surrounded with people and noise. On one side 20 checkouts were lined up in a row, some of the numbered signs were lit and had long lines, others were dark and had shopping carts filled with returned products parked in them.

To the left of the checkout aisles was an empty, unused section with a desk. To the right was another desk similar to the empty one but full of people using computers while speaking to customers. It had a sign which said Returns and Special Services.

Behind the desk was a large room with people on the phone, framed in and with a low, eight-foot ceiling. Hunter was directed to this desk where was he was met by a guy in a red vest who looked a little like young Geddy Lee. He immediately recognized Hunter. "Hey, I know you! You are our champion bowler! What are you doing here? I can't believe it; we have a celebrity customer! What do you need? I will help you find whatever you need!"

Hunter replied that he wasn't there to shop, he was looking for a job because he was, after all, an amateur bowler. The guy in the vest introduced himself as Dale and informed Hunter that he was one of the managers and it would be his pleasure to give him an interview on the spot! Hunter stood at the counter while Dale went into the room at the back and grabbed a clipboard.

While he was waiting, one of the employees (in a very low-cut top… in fact all of the women at that desk were wearing low-cut tops that barely contained their cleavage… that couldn't have been a coincidence) walked over and told him that she had never seen Uncle Dale (explaining that was what everyone called him) so excited before. Who was he? Hunter explained that he was just a student taking a year off school and looking for work. The employee remarked that she had to wait 3 weeks for her interview…

The interview went well. Hunter met with Dale, answered a bunch of questions, reviewed the employee handbook and shook hands. That was it: he would be getting a red vest. He had found gainful employment.

Don't Think Twice, It's alright

S everal days after his impromptu interview with Uncle Dale, Hunter returned to the store to begin paying for his year in exile. He was to report at 8:30am for two full days of orientation and training. It was there he would meet the other managers in the store, some of the people he would be working with and learn how to do whatever he was going to be doing for the next year.

In the boardroom, Hunter was one of twelve people in the class of May 1994. 05/94 Winnipeg South was the designation this class got, each class in each store was identified by the month, year and store location.

05/94 Winnipeg South consisted of a couple of dopey looking kids, four middle-aged men, two pretty but married women and a short, pudgy little man with big fluffy hair and a puffed-out chest. The most interesting person in the room was the guy sitting beside Hunter. He was about the same age with long dreads, a Danzig t-shirt and a pierced nostril.

Everyone went around the room and introduced themselves. Some were looking to get back to work after some time off, others were just starting out in the working world.

Hunter introduced himself and explained who he was... the NCAA title, the Sports Illustrated cover... everything. To his surprise very few of the people in the room looked as impressed as he felt they ought to have looked.

The short little guy was a fellow named Stephano (yes you read that correctly) Rosoff. His grandfather started a chain of 12 stores called Low at Home which competed with Retail Depot in Canada. They were bought out by the Retail Depot twenty-four years ago and one of the provisions in the contract of sale was that his son (and any of his sons) had to be guaranteed jobs at Retail Depot. That part didn't really seem important at the time, but it would be later.

Like Hunter, Rosoff came from a bit of money and had never had to work hard in his 21 years. His father did, starting part time in the summers between university and rising to the role of regional VP for the Eastern Mid-West and Canada. He was respected because of what he did, not who he was.

Since Stephano had never had to work hard, he didn't know how to work hard. He had an expectation of a similar role to his father had but didn't feel it was fair he had to do all of the work his father had done to get there.

For 2 long days, the class listened. Management did their best to teach them about life at Retail Depot, about how to build a career, about culture and values. Everyone knew that their job was to help customers and put stuff on shelves, but they listened anyway.

Over 2 days both of the dopey looking kids were let go. One fell asleep and the other showed up late from lunch smelling of cheap rum.

Most of the class simply listened but Rosoff was very much an active participant. The guy hadn't even been there two hours and was already saying "we" do it this way, "we" do it that way and spoke about things as though he had started and built the regional chain of Low at Home, not his grandfather. He spoke as though it was Low at Home's 12 stores who were responsible for the success of Retail Depot's 600. Mostly, he spoke like someone who thought he was more important than he actually was.

Hunter had seen people like that before, Rosoff wasn't fooling anyone. It was clear that everyone else could see that he talked loudly but was wearing an empty vest!

The Rosoff show went on for a full day and continued into the second day. Lots of talking, constant interruptions and corrections of the management team whose job it was to train him. If it had been anyone else, there would have been no question and Rosoff would be shown the door but most of them were unsure of how to deal with his situation and simply did their best.

A number of people in the class were annoyed by this but it was Larry with the dreads who finally spoke up. In between sessions, with no managers in the room, he made his move as they were all seated.

"Dude, you haven't shut up for 2 days. Nobody cares what your grandfather, your father and especially you have done! Be quiet, I'm trying to learn!"

With that, a number of people of quietly nodded but Rosoff doubled down and told the guy he didn't speak for the room. Hunter had heard enough and could remain quiet no longer, he spoke up too. "Yes, he does! Seriously, shut the hell up!"

Rosoff was not impressed. He was one of those people who had been a nobody his whole life; not one of the popular (or remotely good looking) kids, not an athlete and clearly not gifted academically, all he had going for him was winning the birth lottery! He felt that that Retail Depot was a house his family built, and he was not going to suffer disrespect in his own home! Upon joining the "family business" he gained a great deal of self-importance and this early challenge to the authority he should have been entitled to was not appreciated.

It took him a few seconds to process what was happening. His first reaction may have been surprise but that quickly turned anger and a sneering glare at Hunter and Larry. "You 2 idiots have no idea who you are messing with! None! You are making a powerful enemy on what, your 2nd day? Out of kindness, because I certainly don't have to, I will give you 1 chance to do the right thing and apologize right here and now!"

Hunter took the lead and said he was right; he did deserve an apology. "I am sorry you talked through so much of this class and I am sorry that you wasted so much of our time." Rosoff didn't have much of a chance to respond because Larry also made it clear he wanted to apologize too. "I am sorry… that you are such a clownish idiot and we are all sorry that your dad wasn't out of town the night you were conceived. Lastly I am sorry that you will never reach anything off the top of a fridge without a stool because I left my real apology there!"

Everyone was laughing at that point... except Rosoff. He was very, very angry. "You 2 idiots are as good as gone! I study martial arts, I am a black belt, I am a grappler!"

Hunter replied "I'll bet you are a grappler" to more laughter from the rest of the class.

Rosoff continued, getting louder as he expanded on his initial thought "I am going to get rid of both of you and there is nothing you can do about it and if you do or say anything else to piss me off today... I will kick both your asses!!" (he was 5'4" and both Hunter and Larry were over 6' tall and solidly built, however, neither were grapplers)

What he didn't see or hear was the store's general manager walking in with Uncle Dale to finish the training and welcome everyone to the ~~cult~~ company and give each their new red vest. They did, however, see and hear Rosoff threatening other staff!

Rosoff was asked to follow them into their office and the class was given a half hour break. In any other situation, he would be gone but there was that stupid clause from decades earlier which had muddied the waters considerably.

Thirty minutes later a demure Rosoff was back and so were the rest of the managers. Everyone was seated except Rosoff and the managers. Dale was the first to speak and apologized that everyone had to see and hear that. It was not a good example of their proud corporate culture or company values... that and Stephano had something to tell them.

He looked visibly angry and had turned a shade of red not unlike well-ripened beets. He was forced to stand in front of everyone and apologize to Hunter and Larry for threatening them at work and for his unprofessional behavior.

Hunter stood up and generously accepted his apology and expressed his 'sincere' commitment that they could work together in a more professional manner and hopefully, one day, possibly even become friends. He extended his hand and with all eyes on both of them, Rosoff was forced to shake it.

Larry stood up and tried to shake his hand too. Rosoff initially refused but with the eyes of the entire management team on him, he had to take the high road and shake Larry's hand too. For this Hunter and Larry got an applause and Rosoff quietly swallowed his brewing rage at a situation he brought on himself but could do nothing to stop!

At the end of it, the remaining members of the class graduated. They received their red vests. Their crisp new red vests smelled like fresh polyester and had creases where they were folded. The graduates also got an IN-TRAINING button which they would have to wear for 90 days or until they passed their department certification. For some it was just a way to earn a living, for others it was a memorable indoctrination into the cult of the retail gods!

Down The Highway

Hunter was assigned to the electrical department as they had recently lost an associate who had broken his leg in 3 places trying to use a forklift. No damage to the store or the lift, just the poor guy who didn't think not to stick his leg out as he drove past a metal support post! The poor associate, whose new nickname was Crash, had been assigned to the phone centre which was rumoured to be a place where dreams and careers went to die.

Hunter didn't know much about electrical, but he knew he was tall enough to change most of the lightbulbs without a ladder which made him an asset to the department. He figured that if he could maintain a C+ average at a decent university, he could figure out electricity in a few weeks, maybe less.

Larry was assigned to operations. He had confidence in himself but not his ability to sell or support customers and had made it clear that he wanted a role behind the scenes where he could work hard and keep his head down.

There were 2 parts to Larry's new job. The first was to help customers load their vehicles and gather carts from the parking lot. The second was to pick orders which customers called in and to put the orders on pallets for pickup or load them onto 1 of 3 delivery trucks. It was hard work, but it meant very little time spent talking to customers or stocking shelves.

As it turned out, Rosoff was also assigned to operations. He was originally slated for a management FastTrack program given his lineage. After the incident at orientation, they couldn't fire him. They had to give him a job but there was nothing specifying it had to be in any sort of management role. So, they gave him the most basic job in the store and as HR referenced in their memo to head office, it was up to Rosoff to prove that he was worthy of promotion or additional responsibility. He was given a 1-way ticket on a slow boat to nowhere and it was up to him to earn his way off.

Everything Is Broken

I t was day 1 and the new graduates began their real jobs at Retail Depot. They punched in and found their newly assigned lockers where their new red vests were hung.

Their new red vests were a stark contrast to those worn by the more experienced staff. They did not have such empty, clean vests.

There is a massive culture of nostalgia and pageantry at Retail Depot. There were pins and badges for anniversaries, new store openings, newly added vendors, new countries expanded into and anything else you could think of chronicling their takeover of the world. Many of the longer-term employees wore vests covered with endless regalia, weighed down by 15 pounds of metal, fabric and all of the crap they kept in the pockets.

And on the subject of those pockets:

Each associate was required to carry their tape measure, knife, a pad of paper, a pen and the weekly printout. The printout was a weekly list of products on special, upsell opportunities (if a customer is looking at product X ask them this "insert clever question here" and then show them product Y) which worked exceptionally well. While nobody at Retail Depot was on commission, everyone unwittingly upsold everything. Of course, associates carried many more things in these massive pockets... tools, their smokes or other lucky charms, pictures and personal items.

Hunter reported to the department manager of electrical and began to learn where things were and what his tasks would be. Everyone in the store was given a specific area of their department they had to keep clean and stocked. This method kept everyone accountable from the associates to the department managers.

Hunter got the horrible area of electrical with all of the little switches, screws, parts, plate covers and gadgets. It was hell to keep fully stocked and would require endless trips up and down the ladder to get the appropriate stock needed.

Several hours into his shift he was asked to go help Dennis. Dennis was an electrician and was their resident expert, or so he claimed. He wrote a pick ticket (this was used to show how much of which item was to be cut) for some 12/2 bulk Romex wire and some bell wire. He showed Hunter how to use the spooler and cut the bell wire, also telling him to cut and bring the Romex over to him and the contractor he was assisting at the time.

Hunter did as he was instructed. 25 feet of 12/2 bulk Romex. Cut, spooled and bound with shrink wrap. However, when he handed it to Dennis the contractor said he wanted 14/2, not 12/2. Dennis turned to speak to Hunter. "Really kid? I told you 14/2, go cut it again and this time do it right!"

Hunter couldn't believe it! "No, you didn't, I have the ticket here and not only did you tell me 12/2, you wrote it right here! I heard *and* read it wrong? I had better double check… and here it is, still in your writing… 12/2. Don't worry, I will cut some more now so you don't waste any more of this guy's time arguing with me!"

Dennis did not take well to this. "You little punk, I have forgotten more about electrical than you will ever know and now you are questioning me? 25 years! 25 years!! You are smarter than me 2 hours into your first shift? Go cut this guy's wire and quit arguing!"

Hunter cut the wire and took care of the customer. As he walked to the back of the store his department manager intercepted him and apologized for Dennis. She mentioned that he could be hard to work with and to enjoy his break. When he came come back, she would show him how to sell lighting.

In the lunchroom both Hunter and Larry were getting their breaks, enjoying their crappy vending machine coffee and sitting at a table complaining about their first shifts. Larry had issues of his own. Seems his new colleague Stephano Rosoff assumed he was Larry's boss and spent the last 2 hours ordering him around and getting him to pick the really heavy things (cinder blocks, bags of cement) while he grabbed boxes of screws and small things.

Hunter had a better day by far, other than the issue with Dennis. Larry did not. Rosoff was intent on making life hell and clearly did not mean his apology the other day. He was lazy and spent a lot more time talking to other associates (letting them know who he was) instead of helping Larry and the rest of operations team. Dissent was already high, but nobody expected anything to come of it.

Every Grain of Sand

Hunter was slowly getting to know the staff at the Depot by walking up and down the aisles before or after his shifts. Part of their job was to learn where and what everything was in that vast space. As he explored and asked questions, he began to figure out where all the faces in the lunchroom worked.

He often ran into Kenneth, the store manager, in his usual spot at the end of a long-handled push broom. He liked a clean store, hated doing office stuff and preferred being able to see and hear what was happening while frequently interacting with customers, who loved the personal attention.

Some of the assistant managers (AM's) made fun of Kenneth for this but he had a very personal and unique relationship with all of his staff. More importantly, he trusted his AMs to pick up the slack because it helped them develop and gain skills they would need when they had stores of their own.

The staff had to listen to him because he was their boss, but they chose to like him, in fact they chose to love him. He was funny, friendly and excelled at making everyone feel equally important. His broomstick diplomacy had created a very unique culture at his store and, as Hunter came to find out, a special moment in time.

One morning, prior to his shift, Hunter found himself face to face with a man in his early 40s sporting a Tom Selleck moustache. Wanting to be friendly and wanting to get to know some more of the nearly 200 employees, Hunter introduced himself and explained that he worked in electrical. Expecting a cordial reply, he was quite taken back when the man simply said a very snappy "fuck you!"

Caught off guard and stressed out after a particularly horrible shift with Dennis the night before, all he could manage was "fuck you too!"

The mustached man, Don Roberts, was used to pushing people's buttons and measured new people by how they reacted. He liked the kid, he had balls and pushed back as hard as he got it. He let out one of those loud laughs that sounded like a small mammal struggling for air, where you didn't quite know if he was inhaling, exhaling or simply had a collapsed lung. Slapping Hunter on the back he kept laughing and said welcome to the team kid and apologized that he had to work with "that lazy fuck Dennis"!

Over the next few weeks 5 of the people who were at orientation were let go or fired. One of the middle-aged men had an aversion to sweating as a result of hard work and made it clear he wanted to just be in sales. One of the pretty women was let go for theft. The rest just left on their own, either for better paying jobs or because the work was not what they expected.

Hunter was doing ok except for the regular (and unprovoked) daily issues with Dennis. Numerous associates told Hunter that Dennis was trying to throw his ample weight around the person least in the position to fight back… the technical term was bully. What Dennis had not expected was someone as new as Hunter to fight back. Hunter was on probation, same as all new hires, but he also had Uncle Dale who thought he was a celebrity and wasn't going to let his star walk away because of being pushed around by an overfed electrician.

A pattern quickly emerged. Hunter would be working on something and Dennis would try to make him do something different or tell him what he was doing was wrong. Hunter would respond in kind by saying "NO, I am not going to pick this order for you just because you are too lazy to do it yourself" and pushed back especially hard when he was told off "how the hell could I be stocking these shelves wrong? The spots are filled and everything is in the right place. Oh wait, I did it quickly instead of stopping for a cheeseburger halfway through!"

Larry had seen a similar pattern emerge just as swiftly with Rosoff. In fact, everyone in operations had experienced that pattern as well. He successfully defined a new level of laziness and thought he was their boss. Most of them simply did their best to deal with it, not knowing how much of his talk was real and how much was bluster.

Larry took the most abuse and called him on it every time. Rosoff was still upset about orientation and determined to push him far enough that he quit or got fired. His plan didn't appear to be working though. Management saw through it and rather than punishing Larry, would give Stefano warnings instead! The operations team did start to quietly push back on Rosoff too. They made sure to leave him the heavy picks and nobody would speak with him outside of basic communication of work details. It was lonely "at the top".

God Knows

After 30 days, new associates were permitted to join the weekly Sunday morning staff meeting. Sunday fun day morning meetings were horrible yet at the same time, still somewhat fun at Retail Depot. Nobody wanted to be there: quite a few were incredibly hungover, others were just mad they couldn't go to church. Instead of being open from 7am to 10pm the store was only open 11am to 5pm so everyone who worked on a Sunday worked the same shift and nearly everyone had to work on Sunday.

One of the AM's was a rather soft-spoken man in his late 30's named Joseph. He was quietly religious and often spoke about people in his life or people he had seen on the news and ended it with "I will be praying for them".

What Hunter didn't yet know about Retail Depot was that if the punch clock did not work, there was a procedure to record worked hours. It was called a T&A (time and attendance) form and very few people knew how to fill one out properly!

When Joseph said good morning, everyone loudly sang together "goooooooooooooodddddd mmmmooooorrrrrnnnniiinnnngggg!!!!"

When he asked how everyone was doing, everyone followed with "fannnnn-tassssss-ticcccccc!!!!!!!!!" so Hunter assumed that it was like an old timey gospel church service where the minister (Joseph...who ironically did know all about gospel church services) would yell something out and the congregation (the red vested masses) would respond in appropriate kind.

When he said "Alright, time to discuss T&A procedure" Hunter started to snicker so Larry and several of the less hungover, non-church going folks laughed too.

Assuming that it was still interactive sermon time, Hunter yelled out "preach brother, testify! Seriously, this is the greatest meeting I have ever been to" and went to try to high 5 a very confused Joseph. Joseph didn't know what was going on, but he knew he didn't like it. Some of the longer-term staff tried not to laugh and turned away. The new associates didn't know what to do.

The only thing which saved Hunter was that Joseph's religious innocence meant he didn't know what everyone else meant when he heard them discussing T&A. While he thought it good to be punctual and follow work procedure, he couldn't understand why people kept suggesting he skip certain movies because of T&A. He thought that they were trying to keep him from going to movies about working so he could enjoy his off time without thinking about work.

Not quite sure what was going on, Joseph naturally assumed that Hunter was simply young, excitable and likely in need of saving. He had a quiet voice, but he could speak loudly. "If you are done fooling around sir, I would like to show everyone how to fill out the form" and suggested Hunter sit down, which he did. Hunter eventually realized that Joseph was speaking about paperwork and not pretty girls which made it even more funny to him, Larry and anyone else who had even the remotest sense of humour.

Gotta Serve Somebody

One month into their unfolding careers at Retail Depot, Hunter and Larry had begun to get to know the regular long-term team. The veterans usually didn't get to know the new people until after a few months: so many were hired and so few stuck around. It was much easier to get to know them once they had made the cut: less disappointment that way and it made it easier on those who were let go if they didn't form a lot of relationships.

Both Hunter and Larry worked in departments that had their issues which stemmed back to specific people... but issues were opportunities right? The veterans in those departments all saw through Dennis and Rosoff but knew they were stuck with them, rightly or wrongly.

Both Hunter and Larry were stuck with similar problems, despite neither of them really doing anything wrong.

Dennis had experience and the blessing of Kenneth who thought he was a genius. Rosoff had his family name and the support of HR who were bound by that stupid contract of sale. Neither of them appeared to be going anywhere, which meant everyone else was stuck with them. For most of the AMs who hated Dennis and Rosoff, the ongoing salvos being fired by Hunter and Larry were welcome in many ways. They couldn't fire them but didn't have to punish the guys who kept calling them out on their crap.

In addition to the AMs, Hunter and Larry endeared themselves to some of the veteran staff who didn't like being stuck with Dennis and Rosoff either but had been around for long enough that they knew enough not to make waves.

One of the veterans from doors and windows, Jack, liked Hunter and thought he was a welcome breath of fresh air in the store. He was in his mid-twenties and one of those guys who had it all figured out. He worked hard, was good at his job, a quick learner. Had a nice house he shared with one of the other guys in the store. Their girlfriends lived below them in the downstairs suite and that house was ground zero for several really awesome parties every year!

He told Hunter that there would be a sign going up inviting everyone to the party as there always was, but he wanted him to know personally that he should come if he could. Jack figured that Hunter was busy being a star college athlete but what he didn't know was that Hunter was not allowed on the main campus where all his friends lived, that his friends were pretty busy and didn't call very often. Hunter was quite happy to find a good party since he couldn't go to many of them as most were on campus. So, Hunter agreed to come.

On Saturday night Hunter arrived as the party was gathering momentum, the room was filling up and it was starting to get pleasantly loud He couldn't believe it: almost everyone from work was there save a few. As he was walking into the house, he heard his name being called and turned around to see Don Roberts and several of the other veterans there, inviting him over for a beer.

As far as parties went, it was a typically great one! Probably close to 200 people and most of the night was laid back and fun. There was only one problem all night and Hunter was right in the middle of it. Dennis didn't have a lot of friends at work, certainly none in his department. He did have one supporter though, middle management Ned.

Ned was one of those guys who was just good enough to get to where he was but nowhere near good enough to get anywhere else, ever. Also, his eyes were too close together and it made him look sneaky.

After a number of years stalled in his current role, frustration had begun to set in. He blamed everyone else for his failures, threw others under the bus to make himself look better and turned into a master politician. Ned wasn't there because he deserved or earned it: Ned was simply able to play his managers at the right time and create an illusion of competency!

At around midnight most people were drunk, some were high, and everyone was just enjoying the music and each other. Hunter was walking back out from the kitchen, a fresh cold beer in hand and as Ned walked by, he bumped into Hunter, gave him a little shove and turned to say "excuse me?" as if to blame Hunter for it.

Hunter tried to say sorry but Ned was not having any of it. Instead, he laid into Hunter loudly, telling him how he sees and hears about his disrespect and insolence towards Dennis, how he doesn't take working at Retail Depot seriously enough and how he is just doing it all for fun.

Ned was drunk, Ned was filled with frustration at life and thought he had found someone to take it out on. Hunter was not going to be his victim and 90 days probation or not, he wasn't going to be taking it.

Ned finally stopped speaking and Hunter turned to look at him. All eyes in the room were on him. Nobody was sure if he was going to lay into him or throw a punch. Instead of saying something or doing something, Hunter shrugged his shoulders, walked away and didn't even acknowledge him, which made middle management Ned incredibly mad.

Had Ned been smart enough to do what he did next outside or away from the main area of the house he might have gotten away with it. Instead, he drunkenly did it in a room full of people and in a tone of voice that caused all of those people to look at and listen to him quite clearly. "Listen to me you sack of shit... I am going to make it my mission to make sure that you are gone! You will be marched out of that store and Dennis and I will be right behind you laughing at you! Tomorrow, no explanation needed, 90 days probation!"

Hunter let him speak, didn't interrupt or question him. When he was done he turned around and looked at everyone and finally replied "75 people just heard you threaten me Ned. If I were let go and you were involved, I am sure HR would have a lot of people to speak to before it was approved, wouldn't want it to be personal on your part... nothing would sink your illustrious career here faster than a massive lawsuit against Retail Depot when my dad's lawyer hears about it."

Before Ned could reply, he looked around the now silent room: several managers above him, several at his level and almost all of his employees. He knew he was screwed either way and Hunter had played him. He could either fire him and face legal consequences or appear feckless and weak and have to deal with that perception.

The room had gone silent. He leaned over to Hunter and whispered, "This isn't over, I am going to make you pay for this". His attempt to seem tough backfired though because Hunter loudly replied "No, I won't go sit in the back seat of your car and work this out" and Ned stormed out of the room, driving off into the night with far too much alcohol in his blood.

The room was still hushed in silent disbelief. All eyes were on Hunter again. He looked up and asked if they should call the cops to report Ned for DUI. It was funny, broke the tension and got a good laugh but nobody called. While Ned was a jackass, Hunter wasn't going to call the cops on him.

The next morning almost everyone came into work for the dreaded Sunday fun day. Ned was nowhere to be seen; it was not like him to miss work. The meeting went fairly well until the end when Bob (the easy-going AM) asked where Ned was. One of the guys jokingly shouted out that Hunter called the cops on him for drinking and driving. Bob asked Hunter if that was true and he replied "No Bob, you were there with me, remember?"

Nobody thought Hunter called the cops and indeed he had not. What happened to Ned that night was just a coincidence and a little of his own doing.

Ned had a burned-out taillight of which he was unaware. He drove home carefully from the party, he followed the speed limit, obeyed all signs and signalled all turns. In so signalling a turn, he did so in front of a café where a police cruiser happened to be pulling into traffic. The cruiser, noticing his rear light was out, proceeded to pull him over to politely remind him to please get it fixed in the morning. Ned, smelling of alcohol should have cracked open his windows and quietly said thanks. Instead, Ned decided to get out of his car and argue with the officer who wasn't even giving him a ticket. It didn't work as well as he thought but he was successful in earning himself a towing bill, a ticket and a night in the drunk tank.

When Ned finally made it into work, he explained to Bob some of what happened and Bob replied that Hunter didn't call the cops after all, Ned was just being an idiot and caused it himself. He said he would have to write up Ned for being late to work and that it was the responsibility of every associate not to argue with cops while driving home drunk.

On Monday as Hunter walked into the building to clock in, he was greeted his GM pushing a broom as usual. He punched in, put on his vest and went to work. As he tried to do his job, scurrying up and down a ladder with boxes full of small parts and smaller boxes, he was accosted by Dennis.

Ned knew Hunter hadn't called the cops but he didn't exactly make that part clear when he told Dennis what happened. As a result, Dennis assumed that Hunter had caused the entire situation: disrespecting him, disrespecting Ned, making Ned drink too much at the party, making Ned drive, and then calling the cops on him. Dennis was pissed off and something needed to be done about that kid.

The problem was that Dennis wasn't very smart. Someone smart would hide product in an associate's jacket pocket and let management deal with it when the alarm went off. Someone smart would hide drugs, porn, anything in someone else's locker and let work handle it. Not Dennis though: he instead decided to kick over the stack of boxes Hunter brought down to refill the shelves after a busy weekend.

As he kicked the boxes over, making a massive mess of small things that would take hours to sort, he laughed. He said that it would take hours to clean up and he would make sure management knew that Hunter dropped them and then wasted half a day cleaning them up. Without any response, Hunter got up walked towards the manager's office.

Hunter remembered that there was a bank of monitors in the office with camera feeds. He was wondering if there was a feed of his aisle: he was pretty sure there was. There were cameras in certain isles where smaller, high value items tended to live.

As he walked away, Dennis followed him back to the office and was yelling at him to stop. Hunter only stopped because he saw the camera and had to walk no further. That the man happened to bellow "stop" at the same time was a coincidence.

Dennis told him to clean up the mess away right away and that he would go deal with the managers. Hunter smiled and told him to clean it up himself. Dennis got more upset, Hunter smiled, pointed at the monitor and the security feed of the aisle, complete with the mess Dennis would be cleaning up.

As Hunter walked towards the back of the store to punch out for lunch, he heard Dennis swearing and muttering as be began the task of cleaning up his mess.

Later that day, while Hunter was enjoying his last break of the day Dennis confronted him in the breakroom. He again threatened him "I am going to enjoy getting you" and tried to push him with minimal success. Dennis was a lot of things… lazy… poorly groomed… hungry… but clever was not something on the list of things he was. It was only when Dennis said "Must be nice to have daddy buy you a car. I heard you got kicked out of school for cheating on your exams" that Hunter finally responded.

It was not loud, it was not overly mean, but it was enough. Hunter did have a nice car his dad bought, and he was suspended from school for a year but not for anything to do with school itself. He pointed out that Dennis was just jealous that he had a car nicer than Dennis's and at only 19. It was exactly what Dennis needed; he had his dirt on the kid. Hunter was a spoiled rich kid and he wandered off to tell Ned the good news.

It didn't change how the people who already knew him felt but it was enough to influence those who did not know him and many of the people in their 40's and above suddenly had an opinion of Hunter. In him they saw someone who had everything he wanted for with no effort, a nicer car at 19 than they would ever own, just some spoiled kid who thought life was a joke.

Larry was having no better luck in his department and his relationship with Rosoff was getting worse. Stephano was doing even less work and trying to push the mostly young staff of operations around. Larry ran 3 circles around most of the rest of the team and short of getting caught stealing, would be sticking around even if he tended to push things a little past the point they should be pushed. By that point, he was completely unable to work on the same shift as Rosoff and there was notable tension.

Management had to walk a delicate line. They could not get rid of Rosoff despite him very clearly being the problem and Larry worked way too hard to lose. The decision was made to put Rosoff on the night shift, picking stock for orders overnight for the early delivery truck run. Larry would be given the day shift as he was fast and could pull an entire order in the time it took for 2 people to pull theirs. This did not sit well with Stephano who was used to working days and did not wish to work nights. It was explained to him that his leadership skills were needed at night in the hopes of placating him and helping motivate him to show he could be a leader and not just a boss.

It didn't even take 2 weeks for the arrangement to break down. Larry would come in for his shift to find 50% of the orders not yet picked, scrambling to catch up for the impatient and grumpy delivery drivers who just wanted to get going.

At night, Stephano was even more lazy in the absence of senior management. He had rubbed most of the closely-knit night crew the wrong way and his work ethic was quickly gaining a reputation for being virtually non-existent. He didn't work hard and could not enlist anyone to help him finish his tasks.

By the end of the first week Larry was leaving very simply written notes, spelled phonetically for Stephano. He had gone from Rosoff to Roosif as Larry had started to ramp up in his war against lethargy, sloth and too many cheeseburgers!

"Roo-sif pleeze pick this order first, it is im-poor-tant." "Roo-sif, pick heavy things first!" He even left a very large note in the lunchroom "Roosif, be-fore you eat that next burger, did you pick half of the orders? It is halfway through your shift… did you do half the work yet?"

Two weeks into the night shift and Stephano was simply being referred to as Roosif. In notes, in conversations on the operations team, in signs and even in graffiti. Everyone thought it was hilarious. Someone had even drawn a fat, bloated rat and it had become the symbol for Roosif and found its way onto signs and notes all over the store.

Rosoff did not think that making fun of his name was funny at all. He was upset and registered his discontent with management. With the exception of Ned, who was always happy to be upset about something, nobody bothered to care. He had rubbed most of them the wrong way too. They were professionals of course, but they did the least they had to. So, for the time being, Roosif became a thing.

As the end of September rolled around Hunter got some news he liked. He got to remove the in-training badge and had survived probation. He was still not well liked by some of the staff but got along with everyone in his department and the adjacent departments except Dennis. The Dennis issue had been growing and a pattern had emerged. Dennis would push Hunter, Hunter would react, Dennis would push harder. It was not a fun work environment for anyone!

Hero Blues

October brings about many changes. The leaves, the menu at Harry's, the seasons and the occasional change in job, title or role at Retail Depot.

Dennis was to be elevated to a new role. On one hand, he was a veteran of the trades and knew a lot about electrical. On the other, he was lazy and miserable to work with. So, for the good of electrical he needed to be taken out of there. The timing couldn't have been better: the perfect job had just opened far from the electrical department, and it would rely on his many years as a contractor. He was to work with contractors as their dedicated salesperson. He was to chase business and make sure contractors bought from the red vests vs. anywhere else!

Dennis was part of a test pilot program involving 1 leader in each store and their dedicated operations team member. He was to have 1 person from operations as his full-time assistant and his new role was going to be as captain of the pro-desk. In Retail Depot, someone who doesn't have a full-time management role but has an area of responsibility is called a captain. As an example, there was a first aid captain. Equally important was the party planning captain, earthquake preparedness captain and now a pro captain. While it did not make him an actual manager, Dennis took the word captain quite literally.

On a boat or a plane, the captain is in charge. In the police or military, a captain holds a superior rank. At Retail Depot, a captain (of the pro-desk anyway) got paid mileage for his van, a company credit card for meals and a seat at the board table for the weekly manager's meeting. However, in the mind of the new minted pro captain, things were finally changing. He was getting absolute power and would be answering only to the GM and his broom.

His choice for his operations assistant was Larry. It was doubtful that he knew about Larry and Rosoff's working relationship and even more doubtful that he was aware that Larry pushed back even harder than Hunter did when confronted with the stupidity of others. All he knew was that Larry was a hard worker which (hopefully) ensured that he would be able to do nothing but sell and avoid picking any of his orders.

While a number of managers had doubts about how Dennis and Larry would work together, they knew getting Larry and Rosoff away from each other in operations was a win for nearly everyone in the store.

Hunter got a change of scenery too. It seemed he and Dennis had caused a large amount of distraction in electrical and so both were to get a fresh start, in a new department, far away from each other and from their frazzled and now heavily chain-smoking department manager who was close to departing on stress leave.

At the front of the store, behind the special services desk, was the phone centre. A team of up to 4 people could field the incoming calls, look up prices or info and direct the flow of calls to the correct departments. The store-use tools were set up in there, so was the radio for operations to talk to the delivery drivers. It was not a high traffic area, but it was a busy area!

The phone centre was a motley blend of castoffs and recently injured. There were several permanent, full-time employees, some part timers and a few who floated in and out like the nearly healed Crash from electrical, who had broken his leg in 3 places just before Hunter was hired... ironically opening up a job for him in the first place.

The phone centre staff knew everything about the store because they spoke to everyone in the store. It was hours of non-stop calls and stress followed by hours of virtually no calls... all of it tracked by the master computer. Hang-ups were tracked too and at the end of the day what mattered was that the team could answer 90% or more of the calls coming in before the person on the other end hung up.

These numbers were tracked, monitored and schedules and hours were allotted accordingly based on the numbers.

The team was led by another captain, Terry Nicholas aka "The Saint". Terry was a former firefighter who had been badly injured, losing much of his eyesight in an attempt to rescue a young child many years prior. He was legally blind but could see using extreme magnification and his very thick glasses. He was quiet and reserved at first but easy going. The most important part was that he didn't care about the percentage of calls answered, he cared about the quality of service he offered on the calls he took.

Beulla was in her early 20's and looked like a woman who had just eaten another large woman! She was wearing a tight pink shirt and stretchy, bright pink pants... and no bra. A big curly mop of brassy, unwashed red hair made her look taller than her 5'2". Everyone in the store knew who she was... she would start talking to strangers and reveal intimate details of her life.

Known to embellish those details, she was once again in the lead for the highest number of sick days that year: one of the world's leading hypochondriacs. She had briefly served in the Canadian naval reserves too (in a landlocked city) and only in the auxiliary marching band, while in grade 10 through grade 12. From this humble beginning 2 hours a week after school playing the bassoon, she had become a sniper, commando, paratrooper, submarine pilot and MMA fighter.

While it was clear that discipline was not something she applied to her own life, she did expect others to apply it to theirs. Hunter showed up for training and Beulla spent the first 2 hours showing him how to answer the phones, transfer calls "Are you seeing anyone", look up products "I'm not right now, what are you doing after work" as Hunter quietly tried to figure out how to end the conversation. Periodically Terry would tell her to knock it off, but it only encouraged her to talk more! All said and done, 10 minutes of training took several awkward hours. Hunter already knew far more about this woman than he ever cared to!

She had him try to answer a call but instead of hitting the correct flashing line, he dropped the call. It was a simple mistake and to be completely fair, she did tell him to do the wrong thing. Didn't matter that it was her fault though, she lost her mind and told him that he just wrecked a perfect score for the day!

Terry told her to cool it, enough was enough and to completely stop talking for a while. Beulla yelled at Terry and told him he wasn't her boss, got up and went to take her break. Before she went back to the breakroom she opened her drawer (each associate in the phone centre had a drawer to keep their belongings in) and pulled out a bowl and some cereal. This puzzled Hunter, who had no idea why she had a bowl of cereal poured.

Near the phone centre was a door that led to a restaurant at the front of the store. "Harry's" made great burgers, good coffee and the best breakfast in Winnipeg. What started as a single diner on the other side of town turned into 4 restaurants in the city owned by Harry and his family. He was the godfather of grease and his 47-year-old, twice divorced cougar of a daughter, Edith, ran the Retail Depot location.

Hunter watched Beulla walking over to Harry's pick-up counter where she was alone except for Dennis who appeared to be spraying ketchup on his fries and gravy. She made sure nobody was looking and filled her bowl with the warm, stagnant cream meant for coffee. It didn't look like the first time she had done that either!

As he sat back down in the phone centre, Terry told Hunter to relax and that she freaked out like that with everyone.

Hunter asked why it felt like such a power struggle.

Terry didn't know why, given that nobody in that room had any power. They just answered phones, took messages and listened to Beulla talk about her medical issues and her made-up stories. He did have a twinkle in his eye, even if his eyes didn't work anymore. "Watch this" he said...

As if by cue Beulla walked back into the room loudly announcing "I'm back... did you miss me?"

Terry proceeded to tell her that his mom had just been admitted to the hospital for a testicular infection. "I had that once too, my gynecologist said it was the most painful thing other than childbirth. I had diarrhea for weeks!"

Hurricane

It took very little time for Larry and Dennis to come to blows. Larry was running to keep up with Dennis's lavish promises "Sure we can have that ready for you in 25 minutes, my helper will drop what he was doing and pull your order". He was also growing increasingly frustrated with Dennis's obsession with leaning on one of the support posts near the pro desk... Larry was very happy to remind him that he didn't need to hold up that post all day, that the roof would not collapse if he got up and did some work.

When Dennis did leave the pro-desk, it was either to have yet another lunch with a contractor (sometimes 3 lunches a day which Dennis argued was closing a lot of business) or to get a 'snack' at Harry's. "Jesus Dennis... you eating another burger? What is that, 4 today? How about instead of eating another burger you help me pick some of these orders?"

Other times he would walk past Dennis at Harry's and yell out "Dennis are you having an affair with Edith or do you just spend your day eating burgers and fries? You are going to put her kids through Harvard!!"

At the same time, leaving Rosoff alone in operations was a huge disaster. He was barely able to manage his own orders but took it upon himself to manage everyone else. Orders were not getting picked in time, the delivery drivers were pissed off because they had to wait for hours and they got paid by the delivery, not the hour. Most importantly, customers were irate! Long wait times meant contractors were paying people to sit and wait and when the order did finally come, often it was wrong.

Larry and the rest of operations finally convinced him to take the role of forklift driver for the department. It was an easy job he thought, just spending the day on a lift sitting comfortably. The operations team liked it because it allowed them to get their work done without him slowing them down or telling them what to do. It went ok at first, but he started arriving at his own speed when paged and made the person who paged him feel like he had just done them a massive favour!

He enjoyed being the forklift driver until the last week of October when the sleet began, and he realized how cold and wet it meant being for large parts of the day. The sleet and freezing rain had started and would continue until the snow started. It was going to be 6 very cold months and he realized why he was offered what (at the time) seemed like the best job in the store. He spent long hours avoiding the weather, idling the lift under the lumber canopy (covered area to load and unload trucks) and trying to stay warm while trucks were waiting and products sat. The big trucks were unloaded in the parking lot where there was no cover, and it often took several pages and a manager yelling at him before he went.

This subject was discussed at the weekly manager's meeting and it was actually Dennis who proposed a solution which would forever change the dynamic at Retail Depot. An unholy alliance of laziness and entitlement.

I Feel a Change Comin' On

"Larry is a horrible worker (he wasn't) and we can't work together any longer. Why don't we give Larry back to operations and I can have Stephano as my assistant? He can direct operations and between the 2 of us, we will get the pro customers taken care of. Larry wasn't able to serve the needs of the desk, I think this kid can!"

In Stephano Rosoff, Dennis got an eager and willing assistant who was his type of associate. He respected Dennis and both of them had begun to bond over long breaks and numerous cheeseburgers. More importantly, they both hated Larry and Hunter and both felt that this was their chance to finally assert their authority and get rid of people who they felt did not show them the respect they were entitled to!

Larry was much happier at work not having to deal with a lazy pro captain as frequently. He pushed back on Rosoff for delegating the heavy pro orders and taking the smaller ones. He also continued to push on Dennis who was starting to dislike his new reputation as overfed (and for being Harry's most regular [ironically by eating food which promoted irregularity] customer). They would push others but when pushed back upon themselves they frequently complained to management and HR. Not only were they bullies, but they were also sore losers and victims!

Both Hunter and Larry were sick of Dennis and tired of his crap. He continued to berate Hunter when he saw him and even went as far as to accuse him of dropping calls meant for him (actually his customers called other people in the store for help and had expressly asked not to be connected to Dennis). Something had to be done!

Over a coffee, outside at the smoker's table, it was Hunter who asked how much Larry wanted to bet that Dennis was at Harry's at that exact moment. Larry replied that it was always easy to find him because if he wasn't at his desk: he was at Harry's. They joked about a **Lost- please return to Harry's** poster at first but it evolved into something much better, they knew how to mass produce the real thing.

Their final version of the poster looked similar to what you might see in a post office or police station. They had used a very bad picture of Dennis (there were pictures of every staff member on a mural at the front of the store welcoming customers and there were additional pictures at the back of the store in the lunchroom). It said:

HAVE YOU SEEN THIS MAN?

Last seen at **HARRY'S** ordering a burger and known
to be impersonating a Retail Depot Associate.

Do not approach or attempt to apprehend: subject is exceptionally lazy!

They had altered the picture slightly, blacking out 2 teeth (one on the top row in the middle and one on the bottom row to the left) and gave him a 70's porn star moustache (*the Diggler*). The icing on the cake was the way they cut his picture out and superimposed it on the orange background of the actual Harry's sign.

The posters were done fairly well. Larry was actually a surprisingly talented artist and had he not been the 7th of 9 kids, he might have been able to go to school for graphic design or even marketing. The posters looked legitimate and one thing the Retail Depot did well was printing.

Retail Depot locations did their own printing and created their own signage, printing flyers and literature for customers too. All of this was done in a small, poorly ventilated room at the back of the store. It was staffed by James, a former hippy whom everyone was sure was permanently high from the ink fumes and who they were certain used the ventilation and exhaust fans to expel more than just ink fumes!

One morning Larry bought a ream of paper at a local office supply store and after his shift, printed 500 of the posters in the print room before hiding them in his locker. Other than a few cents worth of ink that James the sign guy was probably going to huff anyway, it cost the company nothing.

Dennis found the first 6 posters in the store the next day. While everyone else thought it was funny, he was upset. He tore the posters down and ran (well not ran, walked less slowly than normal) to the manager's office. As if to underscore his grievance, he threw the posters on the desk and demanded something be done. As all of the managers in the room explained (while they tried not to laugh), there was no proof that Larry or Hunter did it and there were no cameras in that area to get proof. The only way they could deal with it was to catch someone doing it.

Larry's shift ended at 3 and Dennis followed him around for most of the shift, trying to catch him in the act which he did not. When he left, Hunter was still in the phone centre and was, in fact, closing the store. Dennis was so focused on Larry that Hunter was able to slip away at breaks. While walking through the store to find things for customers, he carefully placed posters around the store and went as far as to stuff everyone's lockers with them, all the while making sure to do it where the cameras could not see him.

The next morning Dennis, Rosoff and Larry entered the building for the 7am shift and were met by the posters on doors, in hallways, all over the bathroom walls and even in their lockers. Larry laughed loudly, as did many of the other regulars. Dennis immediately blamed Larry who pointed out that he wasn't even at the store last night and none of the flyers were up when they left!

Dennis rightfully suspected Hunter and immediately accused him of it in front of everyone. Larry and several others pointed out that Hunter was working all night, until 10 and left right after work. Larry made it clear that Hunter was really working... not just sitting around like Dennis did... when would he have had time to put up 100's of posters without anyone seeing it... with 100% of calls answered?

Dennis was tired of official procedure and asked his assistant Rosoff to dig in a little deeper and get to the bottom of it. Rosoff had watched a few cop shows and tried to emulate what he saw but with little success and even less information. Hunter did point out that while Roosif was not only wasting his time with stupid questions, there were orders which needed picking and receiving needed sweeping! Rosoff walked away frustrated as Hunter casually said "bye Roosif."

The next day Hunter and Larry had a day off. At different points in the day, some of the other staff they had enlisted from operations put a few up. When Dennis saw the posters for the 3rd straight day he was incensed! The next day, when they got to work, he accused them of placing the posters and of harassing him.

Along with most of the managers and staff in the lunchroom, both were quick to point out that Dennis had accused both of them numerous times already. When he accused Larry, he was off. When he accused Hunter, he was off and yesterday both of them were off! Nobody else had any doubt that it had been them, but nobody knew how they pulled it off when they were out of the store and without proof, nothing could be done.

The first volley had been fired and the war had begun. Dennis had been put on notice: his crap was no longer to be tolerated and his abuse of other associates no longer went without consequence. The next target was one Stephano Rosoff, aka "Roosif".

If You Belonged

Hunter had enjoyed some distraction with Larry at the expense of Dennis but still had problems of his own with Beulla. Terry was pretty cool to work with and it was easy enough to see that he absolutely hated working with her. He didn't say much to her, he quietly listened and sometimes if she said something completely unbelievable, he would question her or tell her to be quiet. He knew he was stuck with her, and it was best to encourage her to say as little as possible.

Hunter could see why nobody wanted to work with her. Her personal hygiene was deficient: even the cheap dollar store perfume she slathered on could not mask that smell. Sadly, she dressed as though she was 160 pounds lighter, and she did not stop talking all day. It was an endless babble of random thoughts, illnesses and things she had read about or seen on TV and somehow had incorporated into her own narrative.

As an example, she had recently begun dating an actual shaved ape. His name was BJ and he was as close to a living specimen of a real caveman as scientists could hope for. He wore a lot of Brut and dressed in black with a heavy trench coat, like a fat Neo. Initially everyone thought it would be great for her to find a "partner". Ideally, she would find someone to talk to and would no longer burden the phone centre with her stories. There was also an added bonus of ensuring that both of their gene pools were narrowly confined.

Turns out old BJ was an animal in bed and tragically, instead of sharing her weekly illness and fake military memories, she started to share details of her now very active sex life. Many of the women in special services wouldn't even go into the phone centre. Some were just grossed out; others were upset that she had a more active sex life than they did!

Turns out BJ also had some bizarre medical problems like bleeding after sex or urination. (Fellas, no matter how curious you get… NEVER shove anything up "that" hole) This was a very private matter and one most people would want kept quiet but having something to talk about was important to her and so she talked about it endlessly.

Her relationship with BJ was short-lived thankfully. There was an incident… at a bizarre dinner party.

Beulla's sister was very lucky that she looked nothing like Beulla, and through a random twist of fate, was dating Larry's high school friend Jon. Jon was invited to Beulla's house as a guest of her sister, only recently realizing that he was dating the sister of the strange woman Larry kept telling him about.

It was a dinner party, so Beulla also got to invite a friend and brought her Brut wearing love machine. BJ had no idea that Beulla had revealed so much about him, but Jon had heard the stories weekly since Larry started at the Depot. He had told her sister everything, not believing that those stories could be true. She laughed and confirmed that most of what Beulla said was outright fabrication.

As standoffish as she was at work, Beulla was even more stubborn at home and in the familiar comfort of her family. Jon was horrified by every member of the family except Beulla's sister. In between courses they took turns telling everyone to be quiet so their farts would be more audible. As they laughed about their creations, they told disgusting stories and talked in very weird voices, almost as though they were speaking in tongues.

Beulla and her sister were not unique, like a lot of sisters they argued regularly about the most trivial of things and for no apparent reason. What began as a simple enough disagreement about a detail on a family vacation 10 years ago quickly degraded into a shouting match. Beulla didn't take too well to her younger sister quarrelling with her yet again *and* in front of BJ.

As she and her sister squabbled, the tone and subject matter continued to escalate. Finally, her sister responded to one of Beulla's insults with "well at least my boyfriend doesn't have blood drip out his penis after he goes toilet or does it! Mom, Beulla and BJ are having sex!"

With that BJ looked up, looked at Beulla, started to cry loudly, sat crying inconsolably for 6 minutes (which actually felt like 43 minutes) and ran out of the house, still crying loudly. Nobody ever saw him again and to this day nobody knows what happened to him. Beulla yelled at her sister, told her she wished she was dead and ran down to her room. Jon was shocked and left too. He may have enjoyed dating Beulla's sister, but that family was too much!

Later in the week a customer came to the special services desk bathed in Brut. Beulla longingly said "smells like BJ" and did it again a few days later when a different customer came in after a bath of Brut. Even months later she would randomly say "smells like BJ". Eventually it became something everyone just said!

Timothy Burkhard worked in receiving. He was crass and the subject of frequent complaints due to his penchant for letting rip wherever he was. It was while he was unloading a truck on a Tuesday afternoon that he once again broke wind. However, instead of complaining, 2 other people spoke up at the same time stating it "smelled like BJ" and for many years after, it became customary to say that after breaking wind! If only BJ knew how much of a legacy he left as a result of his failed romance.

Idiot Wind

Nobody wanted to be around Beulla at the best of times, it was even worse after she became single. For a week after her split with BJ, she talked about it all day, every day with anyone she could trap into listening.

After the fiasco at dinner (which was CLEARLY all Larry's fault) Beulla's account grew daily. BJ was kidnapped by gypsies before being sold along with a pack of feral wolves. After being attacked by a squirrel in the park (again) he got amnesia. When he woke up in the hospital, he returned to Romania to find his family and a new pack of wolves. She was also certain several hostile foreign powers may have been involved. It is entirely possible that he was a double agent trying to gain military secrets from her despite the band needing zero security clearance and having no access to classified information of any sort.

Rick was one of the younger, less socially developed, guys from plumbing. He came to get some tools to fix a display one afternoon and she talked to him for an excruciating 45 minutes. For probably the 17th time that week Hunter and Terry listened to her story which had continued to get more exciting and over the top as the week had progressed.

Rick never had a girl talk to him or show interest before and so he welcomed the attention despite not really knowing what to do. Beulla wasn't used to people not trying to get away and was very happy to have a willing listener. When he finally left the phone centre, she commented on what a polite young man he was and later in the lunchroom he asked Hunter about her.

Hunter wanted to talk to the guy and tell him to steer clear but to each their own and more importantly, he no longer wanted to have to deal with a horny, single (dressed to attract men but about 160 pounds too big for her outfit) Beulla!

That Saturday one of the guys in lumber threw a barn bash on his property. He lived on his family's farm about 15 minutes from the store and was hosting a harvest bonfire party. As was the case for most Depot parties, everyone was invited and almost everyone showed up!

Dennis and Rosoff showed up together, met up with Ned but otherwise kept mostly to themselves. By that point many of the people in the store had gotten frustrated with them and while everyone had to work with them during the day, not a lot of people wanted to hang out with them after hours. In their minds, everyone was jealous because they were making a big difference. Even alone and off the clock their egos continued to run wild.

Hunter was having a lot of fun. Actually, everyone was. The host had gotten several huge 5-gallon buckets and filled them with punch and some sort of magical homebrewed grain alcohol which had to have been at least 80% proof. It was evil because the alcohol was tasteless and because it took a while to kick in, so everyone kept drinking without realizing that it had a cumulative effect. For the first hour, everyone was pretty much ok and in a span of about 15 minutes it hit everyone at once.

When it hit everyone, the effects were remarkably immediate! Their previously strong and straight legs got weak, and their balance began to suffer. Despite standing still, they experienced the sensation of trying to stand on the roof of a fast-moving car as it sped around the corner on a rainy night! They were not moving but the earth was! The music started to sound really good and everything anyone said was riotously funny!

Over 100 people went from being their normal selves to completely drunk in a matter of moments. No inhibitions, no filters and no way it was going to end well for some of them!

Most of the people had a chill night of enjoyable company. The conversation around the fire outside was boisterous with various colleagues recounting old victories or adventures prior to getting their red vests. When you started at a new job you tended to look at everyone through the same homogeneous lens. As you learn their backstories, people become far more interesting and much more than just a bunch of people you worked with.

Both Hunter and Larry took turns telling stories that night, funny stories resulting with much laughter. As they told their stories outside, one of the guys named Ralph asked which of them was responsible for those wanted posters.

Everyone knew it was them, but nobody could prove it and despite their free-spirited transparency brought about by group inebriation, they knew better than to let on with so many colleagues and managers present. Hunter simply said that it was pretty funny and not a single person there didn't know that if they wanted to find Dennis they could do so at Harry's!

Inside the barn there were a few lights, some speakers and a bar where more of the troublesome punch was being served. There was something for everyone as long as they were there to have a good time.

Rosoff and Dennis were with Ned inside the barn and spent most of the night there. Ned felt the lyrics of the music were not appropriate and was trying to convince the DJ to play some country music.

The barn bash would be a fuzzy but enjoyable night for some and a night of romance for others. For Dennis, it started with Edith saying hello while they were in line to get a drink. She joked that she saw more of him than both of her ex-husbands combined and all 5 of her kids.

He joked that seeing her each day was his favourite part of work. She took this as romantic even though it was only his favourite part of the day because he got some food and didn't have to work (even though he should have) while he was waiting for his food to cook.

Dennis innocently opened a door and the effects of that sinful grain alcohol carried both of them through it. A detailed description of what happened next is not needed, but for the morbidly curious it involved a lot of kissing, some moaning and two very bloated and corpulent bodies getting very close (and possibly dry humping).

He didn't think much of it, but she did and whether he realized it or not, she had found her next man! He was not interested in a relationship, the last few had ended badly. Some men cheated on their wives, drank or did drugs... Dennis used to sneak into the garage at night and eat for hours. His relationships had all ended the same way, with constant nagging and perpetual disappointment. If he wanted a lecture about his health, he would see his cardiologist! But Edith was not like the other women he had been with... she ran his favourite restaurant!

Even Beulla was having a good time. Rick was still unsure about what to do next. He enjoyed having a real girl pay attention to him but had no idea how to move onto whatever was supposed to happen next. He didn't have to though: she was really drunk and while he contemplated what to say she simply kissed him. 15 or 20 minutes of making out led them to wander off into one of the paddocks used for horses. This one had bales of straw on it and was the perfect place to seal their unholy and disgusting, drunken union.

A barn (even one with loud music playing) is not a private place, however neither Beulla nor Rick knew this and were too drunk to have done anything about it had they known. What followed next was deeply disturbing for everyone who heard or witnessed it.

Imagine the sound of a pack of cantankerous hyenas howling in the midnight plains of a wild savanna, as a badly constipated rhino pushes out a series of strained flatulence... a sound not unlike trying to squeeze the last of the mustard out of the bottle for what felt like hours. Once heard, these things could not be unheard and when they were heard, all eyes turned toward the paddock.

Gordo was one of the guys who worked in plumbing with Rick. He teased Rick mercilessly as the 25-year-old virgin. As it started to dawn on people in the barn who was making the sound and what they might have been doing, Gordo said he didn't believe it. So, Gordo walked closer to the paddock to see what his virgin was really doing.

As he walked up to it all he heard was "Holy shit Rick! My big Rick! My big dick Rick!"

Gordo should have stopped and turned right around but didn't and when he finally looked into the paddock, he turned around and threw up in his mouth. He shouted at everyone to get out, gesturing wildly with his hands. Nobody else needed to see that or hear that.

The next morning when everyone filed in for their hungover Sunday, Gordo walked up to Rick and shook his hand. "Welcome to the club big Rick, no more virgin jokes for you!" Rick had no idea how he knew, having no idea the whole store knew and mumbled "thanks"... quickly punching in and getting as far away from Gordo as possible. For years Gordo referred to him as Big Rick and to this day he still doesn't know why.

For her part, Beulla went around the store for days talking about the fact that she too had finally hooked up with a co-worker (there were some of the more popular associates who cycled their way through their colleagues, she could finally count herself as one of them). "Did you hear? I'm a player now!" Nobody wanted to think about her having sex, so most people just asked her about her health or Star Trek to change to subject as quickly as possible.

It was wrong for several reasons, least of which was that it was her and even worse, it was Rick! Everybody knew anyway, but nobody wanted to say anything due to a well-founded fear that she would take that as an invitation to share additional details. It was one of those things you tried like hell to forget as quickly as possible, and store quickly moved on and tried hard never, ever, ever, ever to think of it again.

Alcohol helped too...

My Back Pages

The manager's office at Retail Depot had a desk, a table and some chairs. There were filing cabinets and piles of boxes, some as tall as the ceiling. It had become a small and cramped place with 2 walls buried behind boxes of files. In the office across the way in receiving it was even worse: boxes of receipts and paperwork had taken over the area, nearly blocking access to the vault.

On top of the office was a rooftop storage area to gain access to the roof, HVAC and other important areas. It was filled with years and years of old boxes just like the ones in the manager's office and the main office. The dust was unbearable and the last time anyone other than HVAC techs had been up there was years ago. Ned was given the job of dealing with it, so he decided to delegate the onerous task to his 2 least favourite associates.

Hunter and Larry were pulled out of their respective areas and told to punch in and only to punch out for lunch and again when the job was done. It was a blank cheque: take as much overtime as needed, just make it happen.

Step 1 was to put an empty pallet on a forklift, raise it to the level of the top of the office and pile the boxes onto it, then shrink wrapping them. It was miserable work and it was Hunter who decided to make their lives much easier. They grabbed a couple of shop-vacs and set them up at the far end of the roof, where there were walls on the 2 sides. In the opposite corner, they fired a gas-powered blower for leaves in the yard and blew a lot of dust toward the vacuums. It was not pretty but it did make it much better to work up there.

Once some of the dust was gone, they started to load the pallets with the old papers and when they were done 4 hours later, they had made 6 very full pallets and loaded them on the truck to be dropped off at the shredder.

After lunch, they were cleaning up the remaining odds and ends (old shelves, chairs, display fixtures) and found something nobody knew about: an aqua coloured door. This was not a Retail Depot built store, this was the original Low and Home flagship store: they had found one of its long-forgotten secrets!

The door led to a narrow hallway. Off the barely lit hallway were cat-walks leading to all major areas of the building which ran parallel with the HVAC ducting. In the middle, high above the store was a completely empty room with a full height ceiling and even its own HVAC connections. It was literally in the middle of the store, and they could see the entire store from out of its narrow window slits. It also had a hatch that opened to the roof.

Having no idea what it was for and fairly certain nobody else even knew it was there, they decided to make it their own personal office area.

They found their way out and started to stack the boxes from the offices below in place of the old ones they removed. They were very careful to hide the door with boxes so that unless someone went up there and crawled around, nobody would find their hidden secret.

It would prove to be a very valuable place. As they had found out during the wanted poster campaign, if neither of them could have something pinned on them, neither could get in trouble! This would become their headquarters. Batman had his lair, Dennis had Harry's and they had the secret room in the sky.

Over the next week they pilfered old furniture from storage and even ran a phone line up there so they could take calls, make pages and generally mess with Dennis, Rosoff and Ned. One of the great advantages of working in a store like Retail Depot was that everything they needed was there. Fridge, check! Phone line, check! Cable from security monitors in the office to old black and white monitors they dragged up there, check! Decorated in a way that would make the staff in kitchen design proud, check!

They kept loading furniture and supplies on the fork truck and putting it up there to drag to their secret lair. Most of the managers only saw a couple of associates cleaning up the store and putting a bunch of stuff into storage and gave them a thumbs-up. They had no idea of the truly nefarious nature of their actions.

Turned out to be a cool spot and their only lament was that they couldn't show anyone! It was the little bit of leverage they had against people who tried to make their lives hard, who ran them through the mud every chance they got and who deserved to have some liberties taken at their expense!

All of the managers suspected they were the cause of most of the pranks which had been occurring but of course, lacked the proof needed to deal with it. They did what they could, like trying very hard to make sure that Hunter and Larry were not scheduled together or at the same time as Dennis and Stephano.

To counter this, Larry and Hunter had a logbook in their secret room. Campaigns were plotted out; notes of their work were left so the next person could come into work and could continue a campaign seamlessly. They may not have been the smartest kids in the place, but they had a commanding view for the show of a lifetime!

They started it simply enough. One of them had found a kid's toy in lost and found: a can which had a picture with cow on it. When you turned it over it made a mooing sound. For months, they made pages of that cow sound and as usual, they would be blamed. They took great care to make sure that one of them was around managers when the other did it, took turns doing it and proved that they could get around the rules by working smarter.

The cow was funny, but it was time to use the room properly and launch an official operation.

Someone's Got a Hold
of My Heart

Their first official operation launched from their new ultra-secret HQ was Operation Gold-Burger. Over the course of 4 days, they quietly "borrowed" items from certain associates such as their vests, Dennis's safety boots, hard hats, Rosoff's tool pouch, etc. These items all received a thick coat of gold spray paint and were replaced where they were found.

To keep from being blamed they took items from a lot of people and made sure not to ruin any personal items except Dennis's stinky old boots. He continued to wear those shiny gold boots which smelled like a cheese shop with a broken fridge! He kept wearing them until management finally made him get a new pair citing safety concerns and employee complaints.

Nobody knew who was painting everything gold and each tactical strike was planned so that it would never implicate any one person when they struck. They even hit some of their own stuff to avoid suspicion but carefully left Stephano's items untouched. It worked: between that and the empty spray cans left in his cubby at the pro-desk, he was on the defensive for weeks!

One of the best parts about their secret area was that there were no cameras anywhere near where they accessed it and access was pretty close to the washrooms so all one of them needed to do was go to the bathroom and slip away, up the ladder and into their labyrinth of mischief!

The operation was deemed a success, but more was needed and more needed to be done so a better plan was hatched. All around them were tons of air ducts, some coming, and some were going. They worked in a store that sold plumbing supplies, why not change the flow and have a little fun?

A simple test was planned. The exhaust vent for Harry's would be re-routed to blow out on top of the pro desk instead of the roof. The logic behind this was science: would the smell of burgers cooking trigger Dennis to stop what little work he was doing and go buy yet another burger?

He was already spending a lot of his time at Harry's. After he finished work, he hung out with Edith in the back while the girls up front took the orders. As he nibbled on extra fries and burgers, he was pleased with himself. Edith wanted him more than he wanted her and he was able to parlay that into a lot of free food. He didn't care that his blood pressure was far too high: he wanted bacon double cheeseburgers!

Hunter and Larry had attached a long rope attached to diverters they placed in 2 areas of the ducting. When pulled it would block the fresh air that was supposed to be blowing on the pro desk and would send air meant for the rooftop exhaust to the desk. The rope was hidden in the phone centre which was very close to the pro desk. When the time was right the cord was pulled and within seconds the whole front of the store smelled like fry grease and burgers. The effect was immediate!

As though mesmerized and entranced, Dennis began to slowly walk towards Harry's. It was like a zombie movie, except instead of slow, lumbering zombies searching for brains… there were slow, lumbering, brainless lazy people searching for fried food. Rosoff was also feeling the pull and even Beulla got up and went to order a burger. As soon as they had gone up front, Hunter pulled another rope and closed their burger pipe. The technology was sound, they would use the stomachs of the lazy to control them.

For days after, whenever Dennis or Rosoff were talking to a customer, a manager or trying to work, the rope was pulled, and the smell flooded the pro desk. Nothing was getting done, they kept walking away each time it was pulled. They were turning into Pavlovian rats.

Slowly Larry and Hunter started to think beyond making the man eat even more burgers, his blood would be on their hands when his heart attacked him and stopped pumping! The next level would require some elaborate effort on their days off, but they were up for the task of doing something truly inspired.

Turkey Chase

I n a month when Santa was watching everyone very closely, most behaved in a way that would have made the jolly old elf blush!

Dennis and Edith had made their unlikely relationship work. Dennis was getting lots of food at a very good price and she was getting the physical attention she badly craved.

He was not as successful dealing with his many adversaries at work. The latest dust-up started a level below him after Rosoff started to argue with Larry about who should pick an order. Larry followed up with a loud page "Roosif to receiving please, Roosif to receiving please. Report with broom immediately."

That got Stephano worked up and he went to report to his pro captain with news of the insubordination. Dennis angrily confronted Larry who was filling an order with 2 other members of the operations team. "Why is my order not being picked, I told this contractor it would be ready in an hour!"

As the sound of a mooing cow filled the store, Larry pushed back "Why did you promise it in an hour, Kenneth told me to pick this big order first and then the rest. Just because you didn't check the list before you made a promise doesn't make it my problem."

"It's your problem now, you are going to pick this right now!"

Their failure to align went on for some time. It came to a head when Dennis got frustrated and asked loudly in the lunchroom "In every other store the pro-captain is given the same respect as a store manager (they weren't) but in this store, that is not the case. Why do I not get the respect from you that I deserve?"

"Because you are lazy and blame other people for your own stupidity and incompetence!" Nobody could argue with that point and Dennis left the room to commiserate with Ned and Rosoff. He was surrounded by idiots, and it was hard always being the only smart one in the room!

Ned had become a significant growing concern for Hunter and Larry. He had been pushed a little too hard by them and he was starting to show them that kitty had claws. He tried to write them up for small things and berated them whenever there were no other managers around. He swore he was going to get them, but they were not the kind of people who laid around waiting. They knew they had to take it to him and pay him back for his attempts to besmirch their characters.

On a Friday night, signs were placed around the neighborhood Ned lived. These signs referenced a garage sale which coincidentally was happening in Ned's apartment starting 6am the next morning.

Winnipeg is well known for its garage sale culture with houses competing as to who had the best sale. This ensured that his sale would be a success. Starting at 6am on Saturday morning Ned was awaked by knocks at his door asking about the garage sale. Some people even walked into his living room but in all fairness, the posters did say to walk right in. Poor Ned was caught by surprise when it started and would have worn more than his undies had he known!

The steady stream of traffic went on until well after he started his shift at 11. When he went to punch in, he turned bright red when he got to his locker. There, on the front of it was a small garage sale sign taped to his locker! He knew it was no mistake that people had come to his house for a fake garage sale that morning.

Winterlude

Retail Depot had its core departments like lumber and electrical but there were a number of seasonal ones too. Sales of flamboyant multi-hued lights, over-the-top decorations, shimmering ornaments and the freshest of trees brought a lot of traffic and revenue into the store over winter. The outside plant department was filled with various dead trees for sale and the inside of the seasonal department was filled with everything else.

The area was festively decorated, there was hot apple cider or hot chocolate, and the carols were blaring! There was even a shed with a wood stove inside, for the associates to stay warm between customers. The ends of the trees they trimmed were burned and being as the wood was not dry, there was usually a column of heavy creosote-laden smoke pouring out the door. It was thick and hid the smells of a lot of other smoke, so it was a popular place with the young and old stoners of Retail Depot. Tree duty was coveted, and one could earn a lot of overtime in the smoke shed!

Every associate was requested to take some time working tree duty and there was a contest for the best team every week. Hunter was scheduled to work with Ralph, a middle-aged father of 4 who, until a few years ago, had a cushy union job. Despite this, he was known as a hard worker at Retail Depot and would yell at younger associates who were slacking and accuse them of stealing company time. Ralph really liked Hunter and wanted to work with him. He saw potential in the kid and thought it would be a good way to spend a Saturday afternoon.

They sat in the shed over 2 long hours in between sparse customers, talking. Hunter was bored and wanted to get away to get up to their secret room to mess with Rosoff per the morning plan in the logbook. Ralph loved Christmas and was not going to accept that their time was going to spent sucking in pine smoke.

He confidently picked up the phone and hit the page button "Uhhh… this is Ralph the elf out here in the Xmas tree area. Me and my other elf are freezing our… Christmas hams off out here to make sure you get the best tree… so get your butts out here… say hello… have some hot cider and get your tree! Buy a tree and we will sing your favourite holiday song! 10-4, Ralph the elf out!"

It worked! They were really busy and after they had lunch, he paged it a second time, just after someone paged that cow again. Ralph was able to tell everyone that it wasn't Hunter, someone definitely paged it 3 times while they worked in seasonal, but it wasn't him!

Hunter and Ralph won the contest that week and Hunter got to see first-hand how much fun Christmas could be when you were with someone who loved it! At the end of his shift Hunter was approached by one of the cashiers named Sarita. She was beautiful and had a great sense of humour, laughing and smiling through life. Hunter didn't know her that well, so it was a bit of a surprise. "That was so awesome what you and Ralphy did today. If you like Christmas that much you should come and help us plan our float for the big Christmas parade."

Hunter didn't really care about parades. He also didn't really care that much about Xmas, but he noticed that pretending he did was getting the attention of the prettiest girl in the store. So, he agreed to help out and assumed it would be a few hours on a Sunday morning before the parade. It turned out that Sarita really loved Christmas and he ended up spending a lot of evenings with her at the store.

The parade was a success. The store won the best float in their category and Hunter got to see the result of his effort through Sarita's eyes. It turned out that people seemed to really like their Christmas float and that made Sarita very happy, which made Hunter really happy. So, they pulled out all of the stops and at the end, in the pub after the parade, Sarita leaned over and half-cut said "Thank you for making a magical Christmas parade" and give Hunter a little kiss. It seemed that the exchange of some of this spare time yielded a good return! He got to know the prettiest girl in the store, they became friends and then a little more than friends.

The next week was the holiday party, and it was the highlight of the year for many. To Hunter it was just another party but to the people with families and those who worked very hard for their families, this was a much bigger deal. It was their thanks from the company for another year of hard work and involved getting a small gift like an ornament and usually a pin or badge for their vests. They were also getting a cash bonus and a gift certificate for a turkey!

Ralph set him straight on why it was so important. He pointed to one of the guys named Henry in receiving, told him how his family had to deal with a bunch of real hard issues and were barely making it. To a family like theirs, a turkey dinner was a week's worth of food in one night. It was a big deal for them to get that much food.

Hunter was starting to understand. Working at Retail Depot was still just purgatory for him, but he would most likely go back to school, finish an education and get a leg up in life that a lot of these people just wouldn't have. While he was trying to have fun and make it through the year, a lot of these people were doing as well as they ever would and it wasn't a joke for them, it was their lives and their career!

Simple Twist of Fate

The phone centre was an unpleasant space to occupy when Beulla was on shift. Initially everyone assumed that if she got into a normal relationship (or in this case a relationship with big dick Rick), that she would stop talking and leave everyone else alone. Not so. Not only did they get graphic stories of her sex life with Rick but also that he was not making her happy outside of the bedroom. It was awkward, gross and uncomfortable all at the same time... like coming home to find your elderly uncle and aunt having sex on your kitchen table.

What being in a relationship didn't do for her discretion also didn't do for her hypochondria with December being a holiday themed month for illness. Her latest illness was one she briefly heard about on TV which (if she really had this disease) would have left her bedridden and near death. Instead, it left her chipper and talkative but flatulent.

As a rule, when Beulla was working and the phones were not ringing, nobody spoke. Officially it was to keep the room quiet so that when the phone rang, they could hear the caller. Unofficially (to everyone but Beulla) it was to make sure she wouldn't talk for her entire shift. She would have if allowed and nobody would ever want to work in that part of the store again. She didn't always follow the rule, but it helped a bit.

At 2:43 PM, in one of the rare moments of silence when she wasn't talking and nobody was on the phone, it happened. It was quiet and then suddenly it was not. As everyone was happily enjoying the absence of her voice, they heard something much worse. Nobody missed it: everyone (even the girls at special services) could clearly hear the shrieking wail of air forcing its way out of her ample, quaking ass. It was not that she had to break wind: that happened to everyone. It was that she chose that quiet moment in a confined space to do so.

Everyone else was initially startled and then collectively disgusted by it. Some farts are funny and entertaining, that one was not. It wasn't a normal fart either, it sounded like the alpha male in a herd of elephant seals, suffering from a deviated septum, signaling his dominance the other males in the herd! It didn't sound like a single word or sound barking out either, more like a single disjointed sentence of someone gargling mud while belching out the vowels… a-e-i-o-u. Terry was the first to turn around and ask "Who did that?"

She was turning bright red, first quietly laughing and shaking and then laughing loudly at her accomplishment. Her family often sat around the dinner table (imagine Rodney Dangerfield: when I say sat around, I mean sat around!) and celebrated their gas: group displays were normal to her. She didn't have a lot of social experience outside of her family and didn't really understand that wasn't something most people did, even close friends and especially not coworkers in a confined space.

As she continued to laugh at her rectal opus, she managed to offer the excuse of "Oops, it's my medicine!" It worked for her 86-year-old granny (Meemaw Poo-Poo as she was affectionately known at home… can't make this stuff up) when she used that line, but it didn't work for 25-year-old Beulla with her mystery ailment(s).

The doors to the phone centre were opened widely, the fans were turned on, someone unloaded half a can of air freshener and Hunter made a mental note that the next set of pipes they divert should be in the phone centre pushing the bad air out and fresh air in. That gave him an idea about a quality target for their next plumbing experiment.

After the air cleared and everyone had their say, the doors were again closed and work resumed. Terry and some of the guys in lumber went to a little BBQ shack for lunch: ribs and beans! After lunch Terry was working quietly when a high-pitched ripper escaped his body. He didn't care and he didn't miss a beat, simply turning to everyone and in that same meek child-like voice Beulla used to justify her incident, "It's my medicine, smells like BJ"

Everyone else in the room was laughing. It was well timed and well played. Beulla was not impressed "You are making fun of me, I really can't help it, it's my medicine and don't you dare make fun of BJ... he was a good man!"

Air freshener was deployed, fans were turned on as he continued to repeat himself (quite literally) all afternoon, each time blaming his medicine.

It was a great way to close out another week and even better, the next day was the Christmas party!

Shake Shake Mama

The party planning captain, the events captain and Kenneth worked very hard on the party. It was the company's gift to their employees and no expenses were spared!

The greenhouse was emptied, and tables set up with silky pastel-coloured tablecloths, real (not paper) dishes and a catering company was even hired to take care of the clean up! There was alcohol allowed but only 2 drinks per associate to prevent any incidents or unpleasantness. Cabs were provided and they even paid everyone to be there!

There were a few slightly more animated and lively tables, Hunter and Larry's being one of them. There may have been some empty liquor bottles under a few tables (their table for sure) and while it has never been proven, it is suspected that Hunter and Larry hot-boxed their secret room in the middle of the store before dinner and again after, twice.

Larry brought his girlfriend, Hunter showed up and happened to be seated beside Sarita at their table (she bribed the events captain to put them together) and several other colleagues plus their significant others.

Hunter was surrounded by good people, and it was a fun and magical night filled with laughter and holiday cheer. Many of the middle-aged veterans of the store did not dislike him but were not yet fans and even if they were, the tables tended to be segmented with either entire departments seated together or groups… of younger staff, of the middle-aged veterans and in one darker corner, everyone's favourite associates!

At a secluded table at the back of the room, in the corner, sat Rosoff and Ned who came without dates, Rick sat with Beulla, and Dennis sat with Edith. Their table was mostly quiet but occasionally punctuated by bitter complaints about perceived wrongs. They had all gotten themselves there by alienating themselves from the rest of the staff. Beulla was there for being annoying, Edith and Rick for not having higher standards and everyone else for being mean spirited and thinking too much of themselves.

Larry and Hunter had a few things planned for the party. Just before dinner 6 pizzas were delivered to Dennis's table. He didn't order them, but they came for him, and he took them but then fought over the bill stating that he didn't order them so why should he have to pay for them. Kenneth eventually paid for them and said the store would cover them provided he shared them, which he did begrudgingly.

Then there were the awards. Once a year, awards given out and they were a big deal. Each award was a plaque, a badge, a certificate or sometimes a trophy and each had numbers on them. There were cue cards with info about the winner and a corresponding number so when they read card 24, they gave out the right award… number 24. For some good old-fashioned holiday cheer, Hunter and Larry ensured that several additional awards and a few more winners were added.

In addition to the legitimate award winners, the Retail Depot corporation was pleased to formally recognize the following winners:

The Golden Broom award for minimal effort went to Stephano "Roosif" Rosoff. The entire time he was on stage he didn't have any idea that this was a gag award, mocking him. It may be that he didn't hear the slurred presentation of his award, or it might have been that in his mind he really deserved an award. Either way, his acceptance speech was gracious and eloquent.

The Most Improved Eater award went to the pro desk's own Dennis. As Kenneth read the cue card "This next award winner has successfully conquered both bulimia and anorexia and has shown the world that it is possible to consume 10,000 calories a day and not be an athlete. That's a lot of calories bud! Our very own pro captain Dennis"

Dennis didn't know what to think or feel. Then he remembered: rage! Bitter, burning rage... but towards whom?

He couldn't yell at the store manager for being too drunk to know this was a gag award. It was probably Larry or Hunter, but Kenneth made it clear that he couldn't keep accusing them without proof. He had to behave in front of all of his colleagues, he was in an important leadership role after all! So, in an attempt at being clever he decided to accept the award and try to make a point.

"I want to thank you for this award and accept it not only for myself but for anyone who comes here each and every day and works hard! (some minor laughs from the crowd). This is a victory for anyone who has ever been the victim of a bully (more laughter) and for anyone who has ever tried to make a difference but was prevented from it by the actions of other people (now everyone was laughing both at his words and the reaction of some of their colleagues to those words). I accept this award on behalf of the hard-working men and women of Retail Depot (loud howling from audience, even the management team was dying) and especially want to thank our drunken management team for their support and allowing this to happen." He then threw his award on the ground and dramatically stepped on it.

It got very quiet, very quickly! There was no more laugher, only dead silence. He was being serious, for a few moments everyone thought he was being funny, but he was actually being serious. As he walked across the stage a few snickers still resonated but more than anything else, everyone just looked puzzled.

Ned got the 'acting like less of a jerk than usual award' and Beulla and Rick got the award for best couple... their acceptance kiss was especially erotic and caused several to lose their appetites for dessert.

Kenneth read all of them as though they were real awards, Larry and Hunter made sure he got a few extra drinks before the ceremony to help impair his judgement. One of those empty bottles found may have been to grease the manager's table and ensure that all of them were complicit... except Joseph... who clearly had more praying to do in his off time!

It was an epic party, even the jerks and freaks at the back of the room had to admit they had fun! The DJ was one of the guys from building materials, the Scottish Rastafarian! He had the place rocking, and it was a magical evening of fun!

At the end of the night, Hunter approached Henry from receiving, the guy Ralph pointed out earlier in the week. Hunter walked up to him and extended his hand hoping to get Henry to shake it, saying he wanted to wish him and his family happy holidays. The old guy was not expecting any sort of gesture from Hunter and even more surprised to find Hunter's turkey voucher in his hand when they finished shaking. His eyes didn't well up, but he was visibly moved.

Ralph looked on as Hunter did this. Ralph nodded his head to the other middle-aged staff and beamed like a proud father. The kid had done him proud and maybe he wasn't what Dennis positioned him as originally. He still had a case of Youngman's disease (an affliction that afflicts most young men with a distinct lack of common sense and usually goes away in the late 20's to early 30's) but the kid was alright.

After the party Hunter and Sarita went back to his place and as he lay in bed ~~passing out~~ falling asleep, he felt something he hadn't felt in a very long time… pride. After being upset and feeling down for a long time he felt happy again. The thing with school was not fair but there he was, paying his way and keeping his head above water without his dad.

He didn't like the work, pay or the hours very much but he really liked the people. And beside him in his bed was the most amazing girl in the whole store, if not all of Winnipeg… it was not a small deal.

He had no problem meeting pretty girls or any girls for that matter: he was charming and funny. His problem was keeping them in his life for more than a few weeks. He was selfish, he was young and stupid, and he didn't care about other people. Yet, in bed beside him was someone he actually liked. He categorically wanted her to stick around for more than a few weeks.

He had to admit it: he liked his life at that moment. He didn't have a lot of money and it wasn't the sort of job parents bragged about to other parents at homecoming weekend, but it did something not many other things had: it made him happy! Surrounding him were friends who didn't care about money or things, they simply enjoyed the moment they were living in. It was a way of living he never knew existed.

On A Night Like This

While there was certain to be a party of some sort for New Years, Ned would not be attending it or any other party. In early December he announced to everyone that he and his new 6-month-old shih Tzu puppy (Mr. Boodles) were going on a road trip in his old 82 LeBaron coupe on the 26th.

Ned bragged about that stupid car all the time: it was just ok (it was a glorified K-car) when it was new and had aged poorly. It was a 13-year-old piece of crap. The heater barely worked and none of the automatic features worked. It sounded like a nightmare to take a road trip in the cold weather which gave Hunter a very good and very bad idea.

He remembered as a kid they used to drive for 3 hours to a rib festival every July until 'the incident'. When he was perhaps 13, they took their beloved chocolate lab with them, and the big dummy got into some garbage and filled his belly with rancid pork and rib bones. He vividly remembered the long drive home with the car windows wide open, his mother gagging on the stench of dog farts while his father blasted the AC to try to keep cool in the humid summer night while he cursed the dog! It was a hot, sweaty, stinky ordeal.

No dog in the history of the canine species has been especially good at digesting pork! Pork farts are a common ailment of nearly all dogs, and they could dissolve the paint off of walls! Pork farts would be especially terrible if someone was stuck with a flatulent puppy for hours in a poorly ventilated LeBaron on a cold night.

Ned regularly left Mr. Boodles in the manager's office with a baby gate so everyone could pet him. When he had that dog with him it was the closest Ned came to being a normal person and because people were relaxed around his dog, he was more relaxed around them, so everyone enjoyed it when he brought the dog to work.

Hunter would never have done anything to hurt an animal but felt that in many ways, feeding a hungry puppy something was almost an act of kindness. That he happened to feed the puppy a big bowl of pork fat and end pieces from the deli around the corner was unfortunate, but the dog didn't seem to mind. The little ball of wrinkles ate it up and wagged his curly pig's tail and after a few pets, Hunter went back to work. Mission complete.

Ned set off for his road trip at 4pm. The dog was fed at 3:30 and by 4:30 was percolating. By 5 he was laying them down! They were little squeaky affairs which sounded cute at first and offered about 5 seconds warning before enveloping him in a curtain of stench. Poor Ned, he was in the car for a 6-hour drive with a faulty heater and because of the freezing rain, no ability to open a window!

Due to a car accident on the highway, he spent the whole night in that cold smelly car, parked by the side of the road with the engine running. For weeks after, all Ned could smell when he got in his car were rancid puppy pork farts. It was a rough drive and Ned never had any idea why or that it could have been prevented had he simply been nicer to everyone!

New Blue Moon

As the end of the year inched closer, a poster went up in the lunch-room advising of a party on New Year's Eve at Jack's place. Some people, such as Ned, had other plans but most would be there, many with their spouses or significant others.

The party was like every other Retail Depot party: a blast! Larry was not there; he was with his family and friends at an annual family party. Hunter had put a sign up on the front of the house advising everyone that **this party was 100% Roosif free**. He got away with it because Rosoff was not coming, Dennis was at a party at Edith's dad's house (he had become close to her father and had bonded with him over their shared love of burgers), Ned was trying not to gag on puppy farts and none of the managers cared if he made fun of Rosoff.

Hunter had gotten to know one of the newer hires, a guy his age who played trumpet in a few bands around town. He worked at Retail Depot during the day and killed it on his horn at night. He showed up at the party in a full zoot suit! They enjoyed bonding over their love of music and bourbon. Turned out Mr. Chill was one cool cat! He thought what Hunter and Larry were doing was an act of heroism and agreed to help them execute. He could do things they could not: nobody would ever expect Mr. Chill!

After midnight, a lot of people left. Maybe 40 people remained and most of them sat around a large bonfire in the ample backyard. It was Mr. Chill who pulled out the bong, it was a huge iridescent device which glowed and lit up the smoke inside. After midnight, anything goes and so it was passed around the fire, some took it and others simply passed it on. One of the guys from seasonal was Lebanese and had been in the country for only a few years but by 19, had picked up most of the language fairly easily.

He went to try to take a hit off the bong as so many others had but took way too much for a beginner, intermediate or even pro. He first looked up and said in his heavy accent "This is alright guys? I am doing the drugs too!" Then he wobbled a bit and passed out, falling forwards and right into the fire! A whole bunch of people got up at once and pulled him out: he was very lucky. He got pretty dirty but with no burns or injuries for his troubles. Wisely, he spent the rest of the night safely on the couch.

It was cold but they lived in a town with strictly enforced drinking and driving laws, so nobody wanted to experience a night in jail as Ned had in the fall. A lot of people brought blankets and sleeping bags and slept in their cars. The police allowed this as long as the person was in the backseat and didn't appear to be planning on driving. So as the party finally wound down at 4am people headed to their cars and many started them, turned on the heat and passed out in the backseat.

Exactly one year ago he was with his friends from U of W and on top of the world. A year later he was spending the night with a bunch of blue collar, salt of the earth people and sleeping in his car. He didn't know it, but he was moving up in the world and being around those quality people was starting to rub off on him.

Never Gonna Be the Same Again

The new year brought about a lot of new things for some of the staff at Retail Depot. Many things there did not change and for most people a new year simply meant having to spend January trying to remember to write the correct year. But for several people, life was about to be very different.

Beulla and Rick had not been happy for a long time and eventually they found that being the only people who could stand each other was not enough to have in common. The breakup came as a surprise to nobody: she discussed it quite openly anyone who would listen, except Rick.

He eventually found out about this and confronted her at a bar where one of the staff and his band were playing. Mack McArthur was in his late 50's and a guitarist blessed with tremendous talent. In the late 60's through the late 70's he had a lot of success in the studio for 20 years playing with some great bands like Grand Funk Railroad, Triumph, Nazareth and even backed up Ringo Star once for a solo project.

He wanted a steady paycheque and a pension as he grew older so, like Mr. Chill, wore his red vest to afford his music habit. The only thing he lacked was charisma on stage but if you could deal with him just standing there while he played, you would experience some of the best live guitar you have ever heard.

His band played at clubs around town and usually the staff at the Depot went there to support him and enjoy the show. Rick and Beulla were there along with almost everyone else and at 9:42 in front of the coat check they finally had the discussion that was long overdue. It was loud, it was emotional, and it was over. Both left and didn't come back inside.

Before the 2nd set started one of the guys from plumbing, Donny the human humidor, got up on stage. Donny spent a lot of years managing clubs and had grown tired of fights and drunk people, so he got his red vest. He smoked a LOT of weed but worked hard and had everyone's back. Initially everyone thought he was going to introduce the band but as it turned out he had a lot more on his mind. He asked his girlfriend to marry him, and she said yes.

There was a lot of celebration, and everyone lifted their glasses. Even Ned and Rosoff had to admit that it was a happy occasion. When Dennis realized what was happening, he ran out of there as fast as he could, the last thing he needed was for Edith to ask him about marriage!

Hunter was very happy for Donny and his new fiancé, but he didn't get why he would choose to ask her in a dirty bar with a bunch of people he worked with. Then he remembered his revelation from December and that many of these people were simply enjoying the moment. There would be no finishing college for them and there would not be any future glory. Their lives were set and all that many of them had to look forward to was an alarm clock waking them up and a punch clock greeting the beginning and end of their workday.

Despite the predictable monotony of their lives, most of these people were happy. Life went on and, in this case, Donny was sharing a major event with the people he shared his life with for 8+ hours a day.

Hunter was one of the people he was sharing with. While he took a few moments to realize it, he felt honoured that Donny had chosen to share a really important moment in his life with him. So, he got up and bought Donny and his fiancé a drink and gave them big hugs of congratulations. After all, he was there: why not enjoy the moment too?

Neighborhood Bully

Markus worked in home décor, was quite openly gay and almost nobody in the store cared. To most of the people there, those sorts of details didn't matter as long as he showed up on time and worked hard. He had a great eye for design, was one of those people who would not hurt a soul and would always try to help everyone, even a stranger.

On Saturday night, he was out with a few of his friends when they ran into a very drunk middle management Ned and well-tuned Roosif. Both liked the idea of seeing 'their people' downtown and liked to feel important.

Ned and Roosif tried to get him and his group to follow them to a country bar, but Marcus didn't think they would be welcome in that particular bar and politely tried to decline. The drunks kept pressing and Ned went as far as to tell him that he was his manager and he had to listen to him at work or after.

It did not end well. While Markus was respectful and polite, Ned and Roosif were not, and both spent the rest of the night getting more and more upset. Instead of realizing that they were simply assholes, and nobody wanted to spend time with them, they wrongfully assumed sexual orientation somehow played a part.

For days after they were heard making homophobic jokes and remarks at work which made it very uncomfortable for everyone around them.

They didn't make any of these in specific reference to Markus, but he was the only openly gay person who worked there, and it felt personal.

One night in the parking lot Ned asked Hunter if he knew what he called a gay Indian and replied to his own question with "Ram Das" and fits of laughter. Hunter felt ok to making fun of the lazy: they chose not to work hard but it felt wrong to make fun of someone for how they were born whether it was sexual orientation, race or religion. He knew what he had to do.

There were a variety of forms needing to be filled out by associates on a regular basis and all of these forms were kept in a filing cabinet in the lunchroom. He knew that if he filled out two particular forms and waited a while before filling out the 3rd, that he would be able to create a new associate as long as nobody in the office flagged the forms. It was his guess that nobody at Retail Depot ever assumed current employees would create a new and completely non-existent employee: he was right.

Over several weeks a new associate was hired: Ram Das. And he was to be one of the most successful associates in the history of the store. Over a period of several months, he was nominated for awards in the community and within the Retail Depot organization. It was noted more than once that he never seemed to be at the Sunday morning meetings to receive his awards, but Hunter pointed out that he had to miss them for religious reasons. Joseph was curious as to how Ram always got to go to temple, but he did not get to go to church.

To put a bow on the whole thing Hunter had Ram's paycheque sent to a charity dedicated to helping at risk youths and had done so in Ned's name. Ned was puzzled when he began to receive thank you cards because he didn't remember making such sizeable donations. He was even invited to an awards dinner and had his picture in the paper receiving an award!

Hunter and Larry also had another way to supplement the initial plan. The licence plates in Manitoba back then were black and white which made it easy to make copies of them on the photocopier. Eventually they had the right letters to piece together I M GAY and create a new and very real looking plate.

These plates were attached to Dennis's van, Roosif's Wagoneer and Ned's LeBaron. Roosif found his before leaving the parking lot, Dennis didn't discover his until 3 days later and had driven all over town with it.

Ned didn't discover his for nearly a week. He didn't know it was there so didn't know what people were looking at him funny for, why people were calling him names when he was stopped in traffic and why Markus was always waiting for him to drive into the parking lot in the morning, laughing.

It turned out to be the best form of justice and Ned discovered that he didn't like being treated differently because people thought he was gay. He would continue to be an asshole but decided not to be a homophobic asshole anymore.

He didn't apologize to Markus, but he did start treating him better and it was a start!

Let's Keep It Between Us

Over the previous few months, the word Roosif became part of the vernacular at Retail Depot. The word often had a picture of a bloated rat drawn underneath it for effect. Nobody really liked Stephano Rosoff and the whole idea of a cult built around making fun of an awful person was universally accepted and overlooked. People started greeting each other as Roosif and there were Roosif signs all over the store.

Rosoff complained a little in the beginning but with no success. He was frustrated but management had other matters of greater priority to deal with. Management was also frustrated with him and resented having to keep him in their store, so did very little when he complained to them.

It was only when guys in receiving started using his nickname as a verb instead of a noun that he finally reached his limit. He wrote letters to Kenneth, to HR and to head office about a culture of harassment. They were forced to deal with it.

The afternoon of January 16th became known as the day the rat god died. Both Hunter and Larry were called into the office and with HR there, admonished for their part in the entire affair and given a written warning. The deal was simple, they were not to say or use the word again in any way at work. If they were found to be doing so again, it would be taken as harassment, and they would be terminated.

They were also confronted with a separate allegation from another associate. "We have complaints that you have been referring to Dennis on the radio and paging system as mighty Jabba… and have had mail sent to the store addressed to pro-captain Jabba. Someone signed him up for 31 different magazine subscriptions in that name. Many were gay porn or weight loss magazines. There have been pictures and posters posted referencing his eating habits and someone keeps using clear silicon caulking to glue his van doors shut."

They said they did call him mighty Jabba once but only as a show of respect because they thought he liked Star Wars. They went on to explain that they had nothing to do with the rest of his complaint but could empathize as to why someone would do that to him. They explained that Dennis and Rosoff were large slugs who liked to lie around and get others to do their work for them!

Admonished for their admittedly poor explanation for their actions and sufficiently warned against doing it again in the future, they were sent back to work with a target now attached to their backs. The walls weren't closing in yet but the freedom to say and do what they wanted was becoming more limited. HR was serious and when it was over both walked out dejected.

The rest of the staff were also warned in an official memo and told to be vigilant. The party, it would appear, was over.

Later that afternoon they made their way up the secret room and lamented their plight. The cult of Roosif was one of the only good things about working with Stephano Rosoff. Feeling as though they could actually fight back against his unchecked tyranny and stupidity was empowering. Without their ability to strike back they would be stuck with lazy colleagues and nothing they could do about it! For the time being both would have to find a new way to express themselves: nobody wanted something like that on their employment record.

Something had to be done… but what? It was Larry who first suggest that all Rosoff probably needed was to get laid. Funny as it was, he was right. From there the idea of Operation Perfect Stranger was born. But what kind of person turns a man like Stephano Rosoff on?

Baby, I'm In the Mood for You

Newspapers were contacted and personal ads were placed online for men, women and everything in between. They all said the same thing: come to the store and pretend to be a customer. Go to special services and ask for Roosif, tell the people at the desk that you will meet him in the handicap washroom. The ad made reference to the fact that he would pretend to be surprised but not to let up, just go for it!

Over the next few days, a parade of swingers, addicts, freaks and fetishists from all walks of life came to the store to seek out the alleged sex god Roosif.

Stephano was not sure what was happening when the women started showing up but definitely confused when men in tight pants started showing up for him too. Management was forced to have a talk with him about placing ads inviting strangers into his place of work for sexual liaisons, which he denied vehemently.

When the parade of horny strangers finally ended, Stephano asked Larry and Hunter if that was the best they could do since they had lost the right to have their stupid word making fun of him. They said they felt they could do better and would get back to him. He huffed and said that didn't care as long as he never had to the see the word Roosif again.

Had he just let it drop, he might have never given them the idea for Operation Road Warrior: an operation which would become their definitive work. It would eventually grow into the burn of all burns and took Roosif from being a local joke to an international one. He was going to be seeing the word Roosif everywhere, a lot!

For his treachery and complaining, Dennis was to be dealt with in a different way. Stephano could not be fired so all they could do was make his life hard. Dennis could be fired or even better, stripped of his rank of pro captain and sent back to work where he could do less damage and bother less people. Hunter remembered one of his ideas to use their access to the HVAC to execute a masterful plan, it would soon be time for Operation Muddy Hippo.

7 Deadly Sins

Operation Road Warrior began humbly enough. Being banned from using a word which had become a regular part of their vocabulary was not easy. Having to stop doing so upon pain of termination was even worse, especially when that word was used to relieve stress and reduce tension. They were given numerous written warnings not to use the word Roosif at work and it was not to be used or written by any employees of Retail Depot. Conveniently the warning did not have any reference to getting non-employees to say it or using it off company property.

Initially they simply tried to make the word popular outside of work and locally. They wrote letters to the editor, used it for radio call in shows (they managed to get Howard Stern to ask what the hell a Roosif was) and even had 2 failed attempts at starting a new religion. None were successful and nobody used the word in the store or outside of the store.

Hunter lamented that it was too bad that they didn't have a media budget to get signs or take out ads on TV and in the paper. A light went off in Larry's head; he didn't have a budget, but he did know someone who could help with the signs: his friend Todd! Todd's dad owned a company which leased out space on billboards all over town.

The economy wasn't so hot then and half of his business was with a company known as Moore's Future Distributing. A few months prior, they closed up all of their stores nationally and reneged on their leases for half the signs in the city with Todd's dad. He was faced with a sharp drop in revenue and half of his signs empty.

Hunter found out a little bit more about how sign rentals worked and how people rented those signs. He knew that every road to Retail Depot had a bunch of those signs, and he had an idea on how to help Todd's family while striking a blow for liberty, free speech, cheeseburgers and the cult of the bloated rodent god!

The signs or blocks of signs were leased on an annual basis so when a sign was empty, it was without contract. Hunter told Todd's dad that the more empty signs there were around town, the more it looked like his business was in trouble (he learned that in his first-year marketing class). If it looked like the sign business was a dead medium, people would find other, newer ways to invest in marketing, like with a fax machine.

His solution was simple: supply dictates demand! If all the signs were in use, finding one would be harder and that sign would be in greater demand and therefore drive a higher lease price. By making every one of those signs look used, they would be in demand. It was going to be easy; Todd's dad had all the supplies left over, which Future Distributing paid for. They were going to put tall orange letters on the white background with 6 letters: R O O S I F.

Todd's dad would have normally said no but times were tough, and he had a team of people he was paying to sit around and do nothing. He agreed and the plan was created. They would have teams of 2 put the letters up overnight one night so nobody would see it happening. There had to be a bit of mystery. There were only 20 signs, and it took a full 10 hours. It was all-hands on deck, and they got it done.

The next morning everybody saw the signs and within minutes of starting their shift Hunter and Larry were called into the office and confronted. Both denied it and pointed out that even if they had done it, the signs were off property and not done on company time, per the write up. They were right: there was very little that could be done; these were on private property.

Still, management was determined to get to the bottom of the debacle which had embarrassed them and enraged Rosoff.

Joseph went as far as to call the sign company to try to get to the bottom of it. Todd's dad said he didn't have to reveal the identity of a client, but did he know how much it cost to rent those signs? It turned out each sign was $500 a month so the rental of all of those signs was $10,000 a month! He gave these numbers to Joseph and then asked how 2 guys each making $1200 a month could afford to pay for 1 sign let alone 20?

Hunter and Larry were told that if it was ever proven that it was them, they were done, but they knew there was nothing management could do. They were going to get away with it. Management and HR were not pleased but thought that the best option would be to simply let it die down. However, that wasn't what happened: the word Roosif was about to enter the vocabulary of millions!

A lot of people passing through town wondered what a Roosif was. So many that news reporters started to do stories on the word. Was it a company, a politician, a religion? 3 of the major US networks even sent out correspondents to find out what these signs in Winnipeg meant.

NBC interviewed people to find out what they thought it meant for their morning show. When they started to interview people in the parking lot of Retail Depot, Hunter managed to get interviewed and gave his take on it just as the sound of a cow mooing blared through the store speakers.

Hunter explained: "We are not allowed to talk about it because the person it refers to is a former associate and there is pending litigation. He was fired for stealing lunches and his poor work ethic. He is currently in the hospital recovering from severe hemorrhoid surgery. The word was used around here to describe laziness but in a violation of our freedom of speech, we are no longer allowed to use it at work." He was careful not to use the word, knowing full well that whatever he said could be used against him later.

Rosoff had come out to the parking lot to see what the hype was about: what the reporters were doing there. He heard the tail end of the Hunter's interview and came running over to correct the reporter. He was visibly out of breath, red-faced and sweating, bleating out that he wasn't fired and it was a word those guys (pointing at Hunter and Larry who had joined him) made up to make fun of him because they thought he was lazy!"

His angry defence of character was replayed 1000's of times all over the world. Roosif was no longer a mystery, Roosif became a person: him! Even his mom called him to congratulate him on his special word. The mystery of what Roosif meant was finally solved but for the life of him, Joseph never figured out who or how that word got on all of those signs. Against all odds, Hunter and Larry managed to pull it off!

The word really exploded when Dana Carvey introduced a new character named Cowan Roosif on SNL. The word was used no less than 14 times on the air and the character was a hit! The once illicit word was everywhere... t-shirts, bumper stickers and in the vocabulary of almost everyone between 16 and 45! People would wear those shirts into the store and while Hunter and Larry were prohibited for saying anything, they knew they had won. They never needed to utter the word again, it was on the tip of everyone's tongue by that point.

Todd's dad got a lot of attention from the campaign and within about 4 months of putting the signs up they were all gone, leased to new customers. He even had to put up another 12 signs around town. He went on to have his best year, having been contemplating closing his business before Hunter and Larry walked into his shop.

Eventually, life went on, but for a month or so it was one of the greatest victories against authority in the history of retail. Nobody would ever forget those signs and that word and it continued to be used in jest in that store and that town for years after the initial incident.

Day Of the Locusts

ennis had to put up with a lot of abuse, but he had caused more problems than he gave himself credit for: he caused almost all of his own problems actually. One of the incidents which helped push him over the edge happened on a Wednesday afternoon in flooring. The machine used to cut and roll bulk carpet was not working and it looked like a capacitor issue inside the panel. They could have called a repair company but that would have involved shutting down the machine for a week which would have meant a lot of lost business. Instead, a cheaper and faster plan was devised: they would let their self-proclaimed expert electrician fix it.

Dennis had a lot of experience in residential electricity but a carpet rolling machine is not a home electrical panel. No matter though, to a person like Dennis, electricity was electricity. He assumed that he would simply pry out the old capacitor with a screwdriver and pop another in because in his logic once the capacitor had popped, power would have turned off.

Michael Nussbaum worked in flooring. He was the first to try to warn Dennis that the power was still on. "So?!?" he flippantly replied to Michael.

Hunter said "So? So, you will kill yourself if the power is still on and we will have clean up your fried, grease-stained corpse off the floor!"

Dennis reminded everyone that he had forgotten more about electricity before breakfast than most of them would ever know and that time he may have been right. He had been warned but still stuck his screwdriver into the panel and was immediately hit with much more electricity than was safe. The jolt threw him up in the air and 10 feet back, right onto his ass.

As he got up smoke poured out of his nostrils and ears: presumably other places too. His once curly but thinning hair was standing up on end. He was bewildered and confused as they led him off to the hospital and the power was cut to the carpet machine. The capacitor replacement was easy once the power was off and to the novice non-electricians, it was clear that checking the power was one of the things Dennis had forgotten before breakfast.

The next day Dennis told everyone that Hunter and Michael had caused the accident and nearly killed him, and Hunter responded with "Yah I know so much less about electricity that I finished the job for you when you almost killed yourself. Did you tell everyone here that you were repeatedly told to check the power and didn't because you forgot more about electricity than the rest of us amateurs would ever know?"

Dennis stormed out of the lunchroom and filed yet another grievance against Hunter and after being called into the office yet again for Dennis's own stupidity, Hunter finally decided the time was right to open a second front in their war with against the lazy and stupid. It was finally time for Operation Muddy Hippo to commence.

Dirt Road Blues

In their extensive travels through the forbidden corners of the store they learned a great deal about how to divert pipes and airflow. The exhaust pipe from the men's washroom ran very close to the AC vent pipe to the boardroom. There was a small area they could see down into the room and, if they were quiet, hear conversations. They knew that Dennis always sat at the back of the room at the end of the table, opposite Kenneth who sat at the head of the table. Always sat in the same place, always in the same chair.

Before the next weekly meeting they placed a hidden speaker created from some old speakers Larry had taken out of his truck. It was secured under the table with screws, so it faced up, into the table. A small wire was run to a small amp, also taken from an old car. There was a rope above to divert the airflow, a way to make sound right where Dennis sat and in about 25 minutes, a manager's meeting. The table was set, it was time to serve dinner!

All of the managers filed into the room. It was set to a cool temperature, but it was a small, poorly ventilated room and there were a lot of people. The door could have been left open but some of what was being discussed needed to happen behind closed doors, so that option was out.

Kenneth began to go through the numbers, and it was time to begin. A cassette was inserted into the car stereo wired to the ceiling above and a low rumbling sound came from between Dennis's legs. At the same moment a rope was pulled and the cool fresh air that had been blowing out became warm moist air which smelled like the 4 bathroom stalls below the intake. It was only allowed to blow for a few seconds before the rope was pulled again and the fresh air began to flow.

The goal was not to harm them or kill them and both knew that death by suffocating on someone else's exhaust fumes was cruel and unusual punishment, even for management. The goal was to back up Dennis' rude noise with a bad smell. He had been a bully for too long and if they couldn't expose him for being a bully, they would expose him for being a disgusting pig instead!

It worked, everyone was thoroughly disgusted, and Dennis had no explanation. By the 3rd time it happened he was asked to leave the room and it was Kenneth who ended his participation in the meeting with "and maybe you ought to go see your doctor buddy?"

With the initial operation a success, the possibilities were endless. They had the ultimate weapon and they just needed to find the right way to use it.

Love Minus Zero/No Limit

Valentine's day is fun when you are a kid. Everyone gets a card, sometimes there was candy and there were NO expectations other than to have fun. As you got older the day went 1 of 2 ways: you either had someone or you did not.

To the people in relationships, it was a great day and a chance to show their feelings for their partner. To single people it was a miserable day. A day-long reminder of everything you were missing and definitely no candy unless you buy some for yourself!

The event planning captain and her team knew this, so they had planned several great ways to make the day fun for everyone. Associates could send candy to their colleagues and for $5 everyone in the department got a chocolate or something like that. They could also send valentines to their co-workers. Associates had to buy them from the event planning committee but once sealed up and a name was written on the front, they went into a box and were delivered. Nobody knew who they were from until they opened the card, not even the people delivering them.

Cards were 25 cents each and Hunter spent at least $10 sending cards to Beulla from nearly everyone he could think of to see which ones she would respond to. He also sent cards to Ned, Rosoff and Dennis from some of the people who had come into the store to meet up with Rosoff. *"Do you remember me; I was the guy in the skirt who tried to touch your bum."*

Kenneth got a card from Bob that said "Dear Kenneth, I love you" and Bob got one from Kenneth which said Dear Bob, I love you". Joseph even got a card from Jesus, it was pretty funny (Dear Joseph, Dad loves hearing from you, keep up the great work! Love Jesus) but he didn't really see the humour in it as he heard that stupid mooing cow through the store's PA system again.

It was the card (well about 12 cards to be exact) that Beulla received from Rosoff which made an impression. Many of them were about food and a couple were about Star Trek. Both of these things seemed to get her attention. Rosoff had received cards from Beulla laced with similar themes. It seemed that both of them had more than 1 thing in common. Thanks to Hunter and Larry, revolting seeds were being actively planted.

As the sun set on another Valentine's Day most of the people at Retail Depot were happy. A few like Hunter and Sarita were very happy, others like Beulla and Rosoff were thinking about what could be and Dennis was miserable with Edith. He did enjoy the burgers and being part of the family but all she wanted to do was talk and have sex instead of eating and watching TV. He could still put up with it but wasn't sure for how much longer.

Maybe Someday

On slower weekend days, the atmosphere in the phone centre was a little more relaxed. There was still a job to do but there were often far more people to answer the calls than there were calls. On one such Sunday morning the phone was not ringing, and Hunter and Terry were suffering through another of Beulla's stories.

"One time, when I was 16, I was swimming in a lake. There was a forest fire nearby, so a water bomber swooped into the lake to refill, and it sucked me up along with some of the fish. I was splashed around and hung on for dear life and finally the plane dropped its load on the fire. Out I went along with all of that water and luckily, I survived! The plane flew low and when they dropped me out, I landed on a tree and the end of a branch got stuck in my bum and then I climbed down"

Larry had come into the room to ask Hunter about something and only heard the tail end of it, but he still started howling with laughter. It was a completely absurd story, but she told it with such conviction like it really happened. Nonetheless she yelled at him to get out and told him that only phone sales staff were allowed in there and that he had better start following the rules. When asked what the rules were, she responded that she would be crafting a memo for the next managers meeting!

The memo she crafted read as follows:

Dear friends and associates,

Please do not come into the phone centre unless you have to. It is very loud and distracting and we are trying to talk to customers and doing our work.

If a customer calls us and we page you or call your phone, please always pick up right away.

If you need to get a tool please try to be quiet and not talk to the phone centre staff. Do not go in there to talk about sports or bother Terry.

If you have to go into the phone centre and interrupt our work for any reason please talk to Beulla first.

Thank you - The Phone Centre

She had written it by hand on white printer paper, so the letters were large, and the writing was quite spaced out. She made a number of copies and put them in the box of every department leader and every manager as well as the various captains. She finished it after 4pm on Monday night but nobody would read the memo until Tuesday morning, during the manager's meeting.

Larry saw her putting them into the mailboxes while he was prepping an order in receiving and discussed it with Hunter. Neither felt her memo really captured the importance of the situation. So, her copies were removed from the mailboxes and edits were made before a replacement copy was placed back in the mailboxes.

Her writing was easy enough to copy for the purposes of addition and already didn't make much sense. Some white out and a pencil took care of the rest. What followed and would be found by all the managers the next morning continues to be a frequently referenced memo at Retail Depot.

Dear friendlies and associates?

Pleased don't not be coming onto the phoned centres unlesses you having be to. Its is very loudled and distractioining and we's trying to take to customerses and doing ours workings.

If they customers calling to us and we's paged you or callings your on the phone, pleasing always picked upon right aways.

Is you needed to getting they tools pleased try to be more quietly and not be talking on the phone centre staffed. Don't not going in there's to talking about sports or bothering Terry.

If yous having to goes into they phone centre and interrupted our workings for any reasons pleased talking too Beulla firsts.

Thanken yous, Beulla

Department Head – Phone Centre

The memo achieved several things, mainly ending her quest to take Terry's role and title. He might not have been able to see it happening and he didn't hear her trying to undermine him, but it didn't matter. He was one of the captains, so he got a copy and with the help of his machine, he read it. It was easy to call her out on it and told her if she wanted to write another memo, that it had to go through him first and that she could barely write in proper English as it was.

She had no idea her memo had been changed but when she figured it out, she was livid! She blamed a lot of people but as always, proof would be needed and by that point she was not going to be respected to even initiate a basic grievance with most of the managers.

She decided that she needed to write a proper memo stating that her last one had been changed and that if anyone had any questions about the rules, they could see her <u>or</u> Terry.

She drafted another one and decided not to distribute it just yet, rather she would keep it safely in her drawer up front until the morning but did so in front of Hunter while he was working. Instead of having to take it from mailboxes that time, they would just make the changes, replace her copies and put them back in her drawer, letting her distribute them herself the morning.

The new memo read as follows:

Dear friends and associates,

Lasted weekly you've gotted a memo from me what that was been changed by others people. They people made changes were not by me and we is sorry for then mistake.

If yous didn't had not have any questions, please be taken them those complainings to Terry or my.

Thanken you, Beulla

Once she read the re-edited version, she decided never to write another memo again. She knew she wrote it properly, there must have been something wrong with the copier!

Nothing Was Delivered

ennis had rightly developed the reputation as a very, very, very good eater!

Maybe it was that he was dating the owner the restaurant: maybe it was that he went through a lot of gravy.

There were lots of reasons why Dennis was known as the masticator that he was. One boring Tuesday Hunter and Larry tried to keep a running total of what he ate in a single day. What they saw left them astonished that he was still alive.

2 double bacon ultra-burgers with cheese and extra mayo with more mayo on the side for dipping! It may have been that he just didn't like pickles, but the guys suspected that he refused to order them because they had vinegar, which was an acid and cut grease! 2 orders of poutine, 1 per burger! (Poutine is a French-Canadian creation which consisted of a pile of fries, chunks of cheese and the whole thing covered in thick, rich, artery clogging gravy, best served with ketchup!)

There were also the other orders: onion rings for snacks, the 3 or 4 ice cream sandwiches and because he was clearly counting calories, the 6 or more diet cokes! After spending 15 minutes laughing about how the diet cokes cancelled out the fries, one of them said it was a combo fit for only a pro captain… a pro captains' combo!

Above the ordering area of Harry's there were menus which had various posters advertising the combos and specials of the month. Given that Larry had a great set of skills for graphic art, and they had the run of the asset production area, it was a given that Harry's needed a way to celebrate their most valuable customer.

Over the course of several days and using some pilfered stock photos of food already on the menu, Larry had designed a new poster with the "all new pro captain combo". After Harry's closed for the night Larry snuck in and opened the glass and replaced the current special (the mushroom-Swiss burger) with the new combo.

2 double ultra-burgers with cheese, bacon and extra mayo, hold the pickles. 2 orders of poutine, 4 orders of onion rings, a 6 pack of ice cream sandwiches, a side of mayo for dipping and 6 diet Cokes for only $19.99.

None of the employees at Harry's noticed and Dennis had the menu memorized so he didn't even need to look up to place his order. While he was waiting for his meal, he heard a couple of contractors laughing and talking about a huge amount of food for 2 people. Dennis's interest was generated by the notion of lots of food and he looked up as they laughed and pointed at the sign, daring each other to try to finish it in under 24 hours!

As the sound of a cow mooing emanated from the paging system, he saw the combo but couldn't believe it. How could Edith have let Harry's advertise and sell such a delicious combo, yet one which insulted him? She and the staff were equally perplexed at how such an official looking combo made it onto their menu. Dennis raised the point at the next manager's meeting, at least he tried to. His stomach was especially awful that day once again and after another rich, warm fart, Kenneth decided to end the meeting early!

Odds And Ends

arold Wickham was a long-standing manager with Retail Depot and had been since they were a much smaller company. In fact, he was hired by Stephano Rosoff's father at 19 and had remarked on numerous occasions that it was too bad that apple fell so far from the tree. He thought the whole Roosif thing was a riot but out of respect for Stephano's father, his former mentor, made sure nobody called him that at work.

Months ago, his wife kicked him out of their house. His life had fallen apart as she canceled all of his credit cards and changed the locks. Years spent frustrated about his heavy drinking had taken a toll. The first night he slept in the manager's office but that was hardly a long-term option, he needed a different place to stay.

Above the big bays in lumber were some 4 feet tall by 8 feet deep by 8-foot-long bays. In fact, there were 10 of them and each had a wooden door on hinges on the top. Originally, they were planned to hold nice cuts of exotic wood but when the market for that proved to be minimal, they were forgotten about. Few people even remembered them, and most didn't know that there was anything above the lumber bays other than empty space. Harold had been around long enough that he knew of them and over the following weeks converted the long narrow spaces into a new place to live.

He had a little kitchen area with a fridge and microwave from appliances, had a bed in 1 pod and a seating area with a little TV in another. There was a bathroom area to do his business and store his piss jugs. He even had a pod to collect his empties so he could take them back for a refund.

He had joined a gym around the corner and often snuck out of the store an hour before opening and came back from his shower at the gym just in time to open. Nobody suspected a thing, and he was in the best shape of his life!

This went on for a very long time. Even though they had their own secret space in the store, Hunter and Larry had no clue about Harold's abode and he had no idea about theirs. He was finally busted when a new security system was put into place. The camera locations didn't change but the new system did start to track who was coming and going based on who was using their security passcode to get access after-hours.

The logs often showed him going back into work after 11pm at night and out again at 5am so a private detective was hired. At 11:15pm on a Sunday night he was filmed entering the store and going into his apartment. At 9am on Monday morning, they called him into the office and let him go for misuse of company property and for the empty alcohol bottles.

Terminated associates would be walked out through the front entrance and often other staff encountered on the walk out of the store would not make eye contact with them. It was a difficult way to end your time there, in ashamed silence.

It was not the case for Harold as he was led out. Instead of scrambling to avoid eye contact with the condemned, the main isle was filled with associates and managers, many of whom he had hired. Everyone nodded at him as he walked past them. Nobody said anything as he was walked out of the store in silence but just before he walked out for the last time, he turned to face the store, tears streaming down his eyes and waved goodbye. There were very few dry eyes in the store: even the district manager who had to be there was emotional as it was Harold who had hired him years before.

Only A Pawn in Their Game

It was Hunter who finally figured how to get around the embargo on the word Roosif. Larry was upset about something Rosoff had or had not done. Hunter kept telling him "Bruce, relax!" and Larry kept asking "why do you keep calling me Bruce?"

"Bruce if you could just relax. Bruce if you could just listen. Bruce if you could get around a certain word while saying that word? Bruce if… Broosif?!"

Larry's face lit up like a kid at Christmas. He needed no more prompting. Every person and every page thereafter was the person's name, the word Bruce and then their last name. "Mack Bruce McArthur to the returns desk please!" Notes to staff were addressed to and signed by Bruce. They even changed the names on their vests to Bruce. The best part, nobody got the joke except Hunter and Larry. Their word still managed to catch on with everyone, associates began greeting them with a hearty "BRUCE!" and even Rosoff, Beulla, Ned and Dennis got in on the action.

Nobody really knew what they were talking about with the whole Bruce thing, but everyone was happy they had moved on from Roosif! They spent hours laughing over their secret: they had beaten the embargo. The cult of the rodentiatic god continued!

Pledging My Time

The president of Retail Depot was a passionate and successful leader named Annika Vanderhoeff and she was visiting their store that day. Everybody was on edge, especially the managers. Staff were instructed to answer her questions quickly and not to talk for very long. The managers were eager to impress the big boss and the associates were eager to use their 15 or 20 seconds of conversation to show why they should be in management.

At the beginning of her visit all the managers gathered in the board room with Annika at the head of the table and Dennis at his spot at the other end. They had an open round table discussion which had only 2 notable interruptions. The first was when someone knocked on the door trying to deliver a bag of fries for Dennis. The kid who brought them was a newer Harry's employee and had been told that Dennis wanted them by another associate who paid for them. He didn't know to ask Edith first and instead interrupted a high-level meeting to deliver Dennis's deep-fried potatoes.

Dennis might have looked better had he not tried to accept them, argued with Kenneth that they were there and hot, why waste them? In the end, the fries went back, and Dennis was visibly upset.

The second interruption came just as the meeting was about the end. As the meeting was ending the speaker which had been rigged up near

Dennis roared to life. No airflow diversion was needed: the sound was shocking to her and all she could muster was "Oh my!" She did not visit the pro desk during her visit and what Dennis thought was going to be his shining moment to show her how smart and important he was, instead ended with him on the defence about his digestive track again.

She had brought some of her people from the company head office which was headquartered in Maine. Annika was from North Carolina and had one of those awesome southern accents. As she made her way through the store, she greeted everyone with "How y'all doing?" with that accent and muttering a puzzled "Oh my" when she kept hearing the sound of a cow mooing playing through the store's PA speakers.

When she made her way up to the phone centre the board was quiet and so she had a few moments to talk to the staff including Hunter. When it was her turn to speak to Hunter he didn't wait for her to say hello, he asked "How y'all doing today maam?" to which she laughed!

"Don't get a lot of people in these parts using a proper southern greeting?"

"That's because everyone at our head office sounds like they were bred from a pair of cousins in Maine. I'll bet this guy sounds like one of the Kennedys" and proceeded to take liberties by attempting to mimic his accent. "I'er needer some hourser for the phone centre'er and why'er is our inventory being allowed'er to'er age to 31 days'er?" He concluded with "Its ok, I'm an American too."

She kept laughing, apparently enjoying the brief glimpse of what a normal and uninhibited person looked like. Throughout the exchange, the entourage of store, district and regional managers looked horrified. Hunter thought nothing of it: she seemed like a nice person, and he did not see what all of the fuss was about.

Annika left the phone centre as the dog and pony show made its way to a different part of the store. After they left Bob came into the phone centre and asked Terry what Hunter had said to her. Expecting to get in trouble for it, Hunter simply recounted what he had said to her. To his surprise Bob said that she just loved him and would like to have dinner with him and few of her managers that night. He closed by saying to be good, she was still the company president, and he was still representing their store!

That night Hunter attended a group dinner with her, the regional and district managers. Kenneth was not there which seemed odd to Hunter. Before he left the store both Dennis and Rosoff commented that he did a good job of kissing her ass when she was in the store. He reminded them that he was having dinner with her and would make certain she got the full and accurate account of everything which was and was not working in the store. He concluded the conversation by asking them, as he smirked, how they thought they would be perceived after he had finished his dinner?

At dinner, the conversation was lively and when Hunter was asked to be honest and explain all that was and was not working in the store, he did. He was candid and she listened. She asked her senior managers to follow up in a month and the meeting ended with her thanking him and hoping that he would be willing to discuss other opportunities with her in the future. She also gave him her direct line to reach out if he needed anything. He knew that would come in handy.

Ring Them Bells

eulla's split with Rick was not an easy one. Neither had been in a real or normal relationship before and neither was known for their outstanding social skills. Rick had been able to move on easily enough, simply going back to his old life of work, TV, drinking alone and taking Gordo's abuse.

For a few days she tried to tell everyone she was pregnant. There was a genuine look of fear in Rick's eyes when he contemplated that she could be stuck in his life forever. That went on for a week and finally ended when she shared that she was actually just constipated but for added shock value alone, that she and Rick did have sex, a lot.

Beulla was not as eager as Rick to go back to being single. She was like an animal in perpetual heat except that nobody wanted to help her take the edge off. She started trying to flirt with the single men of Retail Depot again and it was painfully awkward.

Sure, she had poor hygiene, dressed inappropriately, was far too graphic detailing her sex life, could talk for hours and be annoying, but nobody really had anything mean-spirited in their heart towards her. It was easy to make fun of someone whose ego at work got a little too big: Roosif as an example. It wasn't as easy to be mean or hurtfully reject someone who meant well, even if what they were proposing was gross. It became quite a problem as she kept trying to throw herself at various men.

Some guys were rude and just said "NO" or laughed at her, but most people weren't that mean. Some said they were busy, some said they had girlfriends or wives to which she usually replied, "I'm a player, not a home wrecker". Most were so horrified that they had no idea what to do, which made it even more uncomfortable and awkward!

After watching an 18-year-old kid in lumber spend 20 minutes trying to fend off her advances, Larry and Hunter decided that they needed to save everyone else from that same experience.

The first thing they needed was a sacrificial lamb: someone who they could feed to her to keep her busy. Once they had chosen the victim, they could focus on making everyone and everything click. The choice of victim was clear – they had to choose a single man whom they didn't like. There were only 2 people in the store who fit that criterion: Stephano Rosoff and middle management Ned.

After careful deliberation, it was determined that the winner of the Beulla lottery was Roosif the rodent god: it was his lucky day! A plan was formulated to bring the two of them closer together. Many of the other single men in the store welcomed not having to repeatedly decline her advances and agreed to help.

The first part of the plan involved planting some seeds over the next few days – talking them up to each other and helping them realize their common interests so they could connect. Unofficially but conveniently, they had already begun with the Valentine's cards. Star Trek and large quantities of deep-fried cuisine were a foundation for so much more! The next part of the plan was a little more deliberate and part of a greater operation.

For months, as a running joke, Hunter and Larry had taken the tape measure and tool pouch (small bag that clipped onto the belt to hold a knife, pencils, other tools) out of Rosoff's cubby at the pro-desk and placed it in the lost and found daily. It annoyed him and forced him to do some unnecessary walking!

Every morning (in his mind), he had to walk to see those jerks in the phone centre and half the time Larry was also in there using the radio. He would yell at Hunter and Larry and question the rest of the associates in the phone centre and special services, but nobody ever saw who kept putting his pouch in the lost and found!

That morning was to be a special morning. As Stephano walked into the phone centre in a huff, Hunter pleasantly asked him how he was doing? He was not used to getting along with Hunter and didn't know quite what to think, except that he was sure it was either Hunter or Larry who kept stealing his stuff and putting it in the lost and found.

Hunter explained that he heard Stephano was into Star Trek and he had just started watching it so maybe they could start hanging out and talking about Star Trek because Star Trek was pretty cool. Rosoff was perplexed because while he hated Hunter, he was right: Star Trek was really cool!

Hunter had a point to all of it though: he actually did like Star Trek but didn't want to have something to talk about with either of them. The mention of Star Trek had raised the antenna of Beulla too. She was now listening in on the conversation as she considered herself a serious fan. ("One time when I was in the army, I had a meeting with the producers for Star Trek to be a consultant on their show, I almost even invented a real warp drive, but they wanted someone with more of scientific background and I only have a military background")

With a twinkle in his eye and trying to stifle a grin, Hunter got ready to be yelled at and calmly stated "The part I like best about Star Trek is the light saber battles!"

That was all it took! Rosoff curtly retorted "You idiot! That's Star Wars and they are not at all the same!!" Beulla also piped up with a similar sentiment and the two proceeded to lecture Hunter for several minutes and with a level of passion that he had never glimpsed in either of them.

The plan was working. Hunter was used to having both of them yell at him, so he was fine with it but what he was not expecting was how quickly Beulla and Rosoff came together to share their love of Star Trek and their anger at him. Rosoff would make an argument (there were no lightsabers in Star Trek!) and she would follow it up with "I know" and then proceed to expand on that point.

The rest of the people in the phone centre watched the horror unfold. Nearly all were unanimous in thinking that if Rosoff and Beulla were even remotely as passionate about their jobs and working hard as they were about Star Trek, both would be in senior management roles!

As they continued to argue and debate Star Trek, Larry came into the phone centre (having smartly exited at the beginning of the great debate) to ask Hunter to help him load a truck by spotting for the forklift. It was planned: Hunter knew better than to get involved in a conversation with those 2 and not have an escape hatch. They were left virtually alone (as their discussion ramped up, everyone quietly slipped out of the phone centre except Terry who didn't realize everyone was leaving until it was too late). That part wasn't planned: it's just that nobody wanted to be around them for that conversation and left as soon as they could. Hunter returned 30 minutes later, and they were still excitedly discussing Star Trek!

Terry had been there the whole time, every several moments moaning "Be quiet, I don't care about Star Trek!" and it would set the 2 of them off and create even more conversation. Terry would loudly moan and threaten to kill himself but to no avail. When Hunter returned all Terry could muster was "I am going to absolutely kill you for starting this and then leaving me in here for it!"

The plan was a success. Rosoff and Beulla liked talking about Star Trek so much that they continued their discussion at lunch and again at break. Their conversation carried on throughout the week. Then, the most remarkable thing happened. Beulla stopped talking to everyone else as much (though she still talked a lot) and saved her best stuff for Stephano who seemed to like it and had his own brand of bullshit to share with a willing listener. Hunter felt good: he and Larry had helped them find something they both really needed: a friend.

Friendship was not the endgame though. The final part of the plan came together on Friday afternoon. A few years earlier one of the big mega plex theatres moved into town. The Bijou, the older cinema in town, could not compete. 1 normal sized screen vs. 46 massive screens and a moderate sound system which could only cause partial deafness meant something new was needed to survive. Instead of looking ahead to new technology they looked back and started showing classic movies for $3 each.

Hunter walked into the phone centre just before Stephano did for his daily retrieval of his tape measure and tools. As he was walking in Hunter casually said "Hey I just won a couple of tickets to the Bijou tonight on the radio, Star Trek 3. I can't go, know anyone who might want them?" 3-2-1…

Both Rosoff and Beulla jumped up "me!!!!!" and Hunter gladly offered them his tickets.

On Saturday night Mack's band played a great little club called Faces. Faces served <u>the finest</u> pizza in town. The club itself was below ground and crowded (ass to elbow) and when the Depot crew came to party, it was a party! It was a classic Retail Depot party too and almost everyone was there. It looked like their date night went well: Rosoff and Beulla sat together happily, danced together and eventually left together. The operation was a success and yielded untold dividends.

Beulla left the young single men of Retail Depot alone and finding someone who made her happy seemed to contribute to her talking to everyone else less. Rosoff wasn't able to find happiness from work but found happiness <u>at</u> work! He found someone who appreciated him and who he enjoyed being with. As an added bonus, they both hated the same people. Neither had any idea they had been set up and both became increasingly easier to work with for a while.

Round And Round We Go

Dennis had been in his new role for long enough that he should have been bringing in a lot of new business and been a massive asset to his store. The closest he came, however, was being a massive ass and yet he had the support of Kenneth, despite his ineptitude. Most of the people in that store thought he was going to be there for life. It seemed he could do no wrong.

Winnipeg was a union town and a number of people felt that Retail Depot should have a union too. Unlike a factory where everyone had pretty much a similar role and job, the Retail Depot was not a one-size fits all workplace. There were salespeople, installers, operations staff, etc. It was not as cut and dry as those trying to push for a union made it out to be. As Dennis could easily attest to, one size does not fit all.

That did not stop the unions from trying though and it was their closeness with Dennis that finally started to expose cracks in his armour.

Dennis had taken up a conversation with someone who seemed friendly while they were waiting in line to order their Harry's meal. As his new friend started asking about how he was treated at work he could identify with some of the questions. "Are you treated with the respect you deserve?"

Already frustrated by Larry that morning, Dennis lamented loudly "Hell no, I should be more respected by the staff and management who work here. In every other store the pro captain is given the same respect as the store manager (they weren't) and I should be telling others what to do, not putting up with their jokes and abuse about my lunch."

The union rep continued to prod "Is it fair?"

Dennis continued "Sure, I have made a few mistakes". (The same method he used to justify only a few in his head is why nobody would golf with him, his numbers never added up properly, also made it challenging for his doctor to track things like his pulse, cholesterol, and blood sugar levels) "but I still should be in a higher-level role and on my way to a more senior management role."

The union rep was pleased to have an excited audience "Are you hungry for change?"

"YES!!! I am very, very hungry!" (At that point Dennis thought there would be food so he got very excited)

The union guy gave Dennis some of his cards to pass around to other workers. He took his lunch and went about his way. What Dennis did not know was that the union guy was not only part of a radical group of union activists but that he was also an anti-government activist and was suspected of several incidents of minor domestic terrorism.

The whole thing was captured by government surveillance and Dennis had inadvertently gotten in way over his head; his entire life was about to go under a microscope. Things got interesting when two government agents came to visit Kenneth later that day and informed him about Dennis's conversation and his association with known domestic terrorists. Dennis was called into the office and with HR and management there, admonished for associating with the union rep and for trying to help usher a union into the store. Dennis was also told that the union guy was under investigation and that now he would be looked at too. Kenneth ended the meeting by saying he was disappointed in Dennis. Dennis was also upset, he was expecting to get food out of the deal and all he got was trouble, tax audits and extra paperwork!

Tell Me That It Isn't True

What a difference a year makes. Most of the month of April was a good one.

Beulla and Rosoff were on their way to becoming a couple and leaving everyone else alone.

The word Bruce became a new way of fighting back against authority and laziness; Hunter and Larry made a point of using it often and along the way they had dragged everyone along into their madness.

Hunter gained the ear of the president of Retail Depot.

Dennis accidently started to associate with some questionable people and the myth of the Teflon pro captain began to unwind.

But it was how April ended which everyone remembered.

Everyone was out at The Residence, another great dive bar that Mack's band had filled. It was like almost every other night until one of the bouncers came over to Ralph and told him that he had a phone call. When Ralph came back, he was crying, it was his mom: his dad had died suddenly.

When someone loses a parent, a sibling, a spouse… anyone important, they are at their weakest and so emotionally vulnerable. For many, being a man means you are not supposed to show your real emotions. Yet here was one of the toughest guys in the store, bawling his eyes out in a room full of people. Other people were crying too; he was not the only one who had suffered the pain of losing a parent and no matter how long it had been, the pain was always raw and just under the surface. Ralph was suffering, but he was not suffering alone, and he was around other people who cared about him and understood his loss.

He went outside and sat on a bench crying, waiting for his wife to come pick him up to take him to see his mom. That next week was hard on Ralph. Work let him take a few weeks off and during the first week he was never alone. A lifetime of being a good person had resulted in a lot of people who loved him and wanted to support him. Friends from every stage of his life were there for him, including his friends at Retail Depot.

There were cards and flowers but there were also dinners, visits and sometimes, a shoulder to cry on. In spending some time with Ralph, Hunter saw a fragile man who was mourning a huge loss and yet was still somewhat in shock. As they spoke, he lamented all of the things he wished he had been able to say to his dad and that he still couldn't believe he was gone.

Then he pulled himself together and looked at Hunter, his watery eyes were red and bloodshot. "Kid, you see this? I have more than 20 years on you, and I still didn't say what I wanted to dad and we never did agree on so many things. Don't make this mistake" and he sat down crying again.

Hunter hadn't spoken to or with his dad at all in nearly a year. His dad knew he had been suspended from school and was still living in Winnipeg but very little else. He was disappointed but not upset, mostly he was concerned for Hunter. He missed his son. Hoping Hunter was well, he kept hoping he would call him to let him know he was ok.

Hunter saw himself in 20 years sitting on a similar couch with similar regrets, so that night, after he left Ralph's, he called his father. It was not a long call, but he said he was working, was doing well and would try to come see him soon. He was glad he made that call, so was his father. At least they were talking again.

Tragedy Of the Trade

While there were those who made fun of Kenneth for his partnership with the broom and for often being too hands-off and letting his managers run the store, there were others who sought his successful formula to create a similar culture in other stores. His store always got very high scores for customer service in surveys.

In May, Kenneth was to be given a massive opportunity to move from managing a store to helping the next generation of managers develop. In true Retail Depot fashion, a party was held and because it was Kenneth, almost everyone was there.

It was one of the better parties and was held at the home of Jamie, one of the assistant managers. He was still finishing his basement, so his garage was stacked with drywall. Much of the staff hung out in the backyard where Kenneth held court. A few smart people had slipped away to the garage to get a break from some of the people in the backyard.

Nobody really remembers who lit the first joint, but several made their way around the circle and a dense cloud formed in the poorly ventilated space. At one point Jamie came out to see what was going on and looked longingly at the circle. When asked if he wanted to join, he muttered that he could not be seen at a work party smoking up with the staff... but then he smiled and said he was only standing there but he wasn't going to hit it, even once. The fact that he only needed to stand with them for five minutes to get a secondary was not mentioned but everybody knew why he stood there for close to 45 minutes before returning to the backyard!

Kenneth's last day was a sad one, but in retail, life goes on. His replacement was Gregor Henderson who had a reputation of gutting stores, the wholesale firing of associates and sterilizing store culture. His job was to drive results and he would do whatever it took to get there. People were on edge and not everyone was as happy to meet him as they should have been.

Within minutes of his arrival at the store he was mobbed. Assistant managers needed him to approve time-sensitive decisions and sign off on numerous things. Department managers wanted to make a strong first impression and a certain pro captain decided to position himself as an informal assistant manager.

It was pretty standard stuff for the first few days until he started to call employees into the office and review their last 6 months of work. He did this with all staff and with the troublemakers like Hunter and Larry it came with a stern warning to do better there or keep doing what they had been doing someplace else. Without the proper context, a lot of those write ups did make them look pretty bad.

Up until that point there had been some detente, the store manager was off limits for pranks, but that was before Gregor fired the first shots in a war he had no idea was coming. Everyone had a good relationship with Kenneth, but he let them get away with a lot more than Gregor would. He may currently manage the store, but it was still their store: he was just visiting!

Some like Ned and Rosoff worked very hard to ingratiate themselves with Gregor and with a blank slate they had a very good opportunity to do so. They made sure to let him know that they were looking forward to working with him to bring some much-needed changes to the store and working with him to get rid of childish games and harassment, rather conveniently omitting their parts in many of the conflicts over the last year.

Beulla lasted 2 minutes with Gregor in what should have been a 30-minute review. He had only needed to watch and listen to her in the lunchroom for the briefest of moments to know to cut their meeting short. He pre-arranged a call to him a few minutes after they began that required his attention. He apologized and said he had to reschedule.

It was a polite way of avoiding a conversation with her, you had to hand that to him, but what could have been only 30 painful minutes ended up being months of Beulla <u>hounding</u> him! Starting later that day and for many months she did not leave him alone. She called him, she apprehended him in the aisles, she asked about it during her review, she bugged him in the lunchroom and left regular notes in his mailbox.

Given that her life was an open book, it did not take her long to let almost everyone know that she really wanted to speak to Gregor and was not going to let up until she did. After that it became a lot easier to end one of her stories or get her to leave the phone centre. It didn't matter what she was talking about, if you said "Oh Beulla, Gregor was looking for you: wanted to talk to you about something" she took off as fast as she could!

It did not matter whether he was in a meeting, another conversation or simply doing something else. Beulla stalked him everywhere. Once she even followed him into the bathroom.

She would burst into the office and loudly proclaim "You wanted to see me? Here I am!!" and he would politely decline by saying "Oh hey, I am actually in the middle of something, maybe we can arrange some time later?" It was nice and he was trying to be mindful of her feelings, but he did himself no favours and as a result, she did not let him alone for months!

Dennis found himself on the hot seat very quickly. While under Kenneth's regime he enjoyed feeling like an important manager, Gregor did not differentiate between him and the guy who planned the parties or did first aid. The change was not easy on Dennis. He had gone from ordering everyone around to being told that the department leaders were above him in seniority and he technically had to take orders from them!

His relationship didn't get any better when the speaker under the table and bathroom exhaust fumes were introduced to Gregor as Dennis's bad digestion in a manager's meeting. It continued to get worse because each time Dennis went up to Harry's for a snack, Gregor followed him and asked him how it was that he only had 2 fifteen-minute breaks but clocked close to an hour just at Harry's alone and even more time in the lunchroom.

Gregor had one thing going for him: he didn't care about anyone at the store and had no history with any of them. He was able to call it as he saw it and he saw right through Dennis right away!

Not everyone suffered as much. Hunter and Larry still caused a lot of trouble in the store but smartly managed to stay under his radar. Dennis was dealing with a very rapid fall from grace and in a sign that the apocalypse was coming, Ned and Rosoff were respected! For the time being they were on Gregor's good list and his kind of associates. They took direction from their manager; they were company men, and they didn't care about people... they cared about results.

The people who suffered most were the hard-working people who had toiled loyally for years and done nothing wrong. There are 2 ways to get what you want from people: either build them up or break them down. Gregor liked to break people down. When you have been doing a job as instructed and some new person comes in to tear everything you are used to, apart, it hurts.

Grown men like Ralph, Mack and Henry were publicly insulted and berated when they didn't answer his questions the way he wanted them answered. It was not right and too many hard-working people had to suffer through that dressing down.

It took him very little time to make nearly everyone at the store miserable. He fired several associates as well as a department head and even a recently transferred assistant manager. Good people who had done nothing wrong, they were just made examples of to bring everyone else in line.

The staff had a special culture and were a successful store, yet there was a new guy who not only knew everything but felt their success was a fluke and not a result of the people who were the heart and soul of the store. The store itself was just a bunch of shelves and products: an empty shell filled with goods. What gave the store its soul was its people. This was their store; Retail Depot may have owned it, but it was their store.

Something would have to be done!

You Own a Racehorse

Seven days. That was how long it took Gregor to completely undo the successful mix of people it took Kenneth years to create. A lot of people had been rubbed the wrong way and any pranks or pratfalls directed at him would be viewed as heroic by the majority of the staff, save the usual few malcontents and complainers.

At the end of his first week, it began: **Operation Cheese Wheel**. As had happened to Dennis, as had happened to Roosif and Ned... also happened to Gregor. It was his decision through: he choose not to subscribe to the basic concept of showing proper respect for others, regardless of position or authority. When it began, he still thought it was his store: the next few weeks would remind him that he just ran it - that store belonged to the people who kept it going each and every day!

Gregor considered himself a car guy and was especially proud of his 'hot rod': a 1984 Mustang hatchback. Loved was an understatement. He spent a small fortune customizing the car but given the year and design, he would have been just as well-served customizing a Dodge Dart or Ned's shitty old LeBaron.

He had installed a huge spoiler, a muffler that made it sound like a broken-down Tercel and a large decal across the front window of a dog biting a bone and the words "NO SURRENDER!!!" complete with multiple explanation points. It looked like the kind of car skeezy nineteen-year-olds drove to try to pick up high school girls at crappy strip malls.

He had made it very clear that the parking spot at the end of the employee parking lot, closest to the store, was now exclusively the store manager's parking spot. Until then it was reserved for the employee of the month and when they lost it, the staff were justifiably upset. It was one of their few perks and now it was gone too. He even had the store produce a sign that said it was only for him to park in and all others would be towed.

It was with that spot and that car that a statement would be made.

It began innocently enough. The arriving transport trucks full of lumber, assorted skids of fence panels, tubs and other bulky items were unloaded in the parking lot and brought into the store. Those trucks blocked almost all views of the parking lot from the store. That would be the key: forklifts and big trucks running cover.

The first few days were pretty simple: pick up his car with the forklift and moving it from his coveted spot to another nearby. The first time it happened he was perplexed and didn't really catch on. The second time he was livid and tried to find out who had done it. He questioned all of the staff, and all said the same thing: yes, they had seen a bunch of forklifts buzzing around as they unloaded the truck but nothing else.

For several days after, the car found its way into customer parking, fire lanes, wheelchair only spots and often blocking access to the lumber doors. He opened a work order to have a camera installed but the request would have to be approved by HQ and that could take months.

The following week when Gregor pulled into the parking lot, he was dismayed to find 2 skids of 2x4x8 lumber stacked in his spot.

The following day when he came out to get in his car at the end of the day his car was surrounded by skids of lumber on all sides.

On Saturday afternoon, he looked out and was pleased to see no lumber around his car. When he got closer, he did get very angry when he noticed that his car was shrink-wrapped tightly!

Larry happened across the exact same car as Gregor drove at the local wreckers while searching for new bucket seats for his truck. The colour and style were right, and their original plan was to buy it and drive it to work to mock his: however, it was not going to work because by the time they decided to buy it and plan the operation, that car has already been picked clean and crushed.

The plan had to change, and it actually got better: they worked out a deal with the guy at the wreckers and would take the car in the morning and return it later for only a case of beer. They loaded it onto a trailer Larry brought from his parents' house. When Gregor was in a meeting, they used the forklift to move Gregor's car to the customer parking area where he would find it, but not right away. They even took his personalized plates off his still ok car and put them on the wreck. Then they dropped the wreck into his spot and went back to work: no need to watch it happen... they would know, the whole store would know!

When Gregor went to have his cigarette and check on his car, he couldn't see it at first because it was blocked by yet another lumber truck. However, when he got closer he dropped his coffee on the ground and his cigarette too. There, in his spot, was his prized 84 Mustang... complete with his AZZKIKR plates... completely destroyed! He was livid, cops would be called... people would be fired... he would fire the entire store if he had to!

When the cops came, they drove around the lot once and found his car parked in customer parking. They left after confirming that it was his car and telling him to get the plates back on because technically it was uninsured should something happen to it.

As usual there was no witness to the crime: nobody saw a thing. He was hated, nobody cared, and a lot of people would be happy if his car was destroyed in the process!

The following week when he tried to go home, he noticed his car was not in its spot at all. There was a sign directing him to go to lumber where he found another sign directing him to look up. There was his car on the roof! In a very high pitched and aggravated tone of voice all he could manage was "Why? Why? What the hell? My car... why my car?!"

He had no idea how they got it up there, but he was once again ready to fire the whole store! As before, nobody saw a thing and he had no idea how to stop the endless abuse. He waited an hour for the lumber staff to get his car down. Took lumber a while because they had no idea how it got up there, having "forgotten" how Hunter had lifted the car with a smaller forklift, while Larry used the big forklift to lift Hunter's lift so it could place the car on the roof.

The final straw which caused Gregor to start driving his Civic and leaving his muscle-like car home was vintage retail terrorism. It involved Dennis and Gregor… for only a little extra effort and planning they got 2 for the price of 1. **Operation Hood Ornament** was about to commence.

It began when Gregor stopped parking out front and had taken to parking his prized Mustang in one of the unused receiving bays. He had left orders for Receiving to only use bays 1 and 2 to allow them to watch the car in bay 3 and keep bay door 3 open, even if it was cold out. The only time they were allowed to close the doors was when they went for lunch between 12 and 1pm. It was company policy that all doors were locked at that time. The receiving staff were not fans of the open-door policy nor having to babysit his car.

It took Hunter, Larry and even some eager associates (some of whom had previously said they spent too much time fooling around at work) about a week to pull together. A lot of otherwise well-behaved staff who took up arms did so to strike a blow for decency and righteousness, pre-building many of the required props needed and storing them innocuously at the side of the building.

On the day of execution, they had to move fast as there were a number of moving pieces.

Literally.

Step 1

Get the laxatives into Dennis. It was easy, they melted chocolate and made cookies for him to eat, which may have also contained a micro-dose of mushrooms as well. The directions on the box recommended that he eat no more than a 10mg dose every 24 hours for optimal effectiveness. They used and fed him the whole box, all 500 grams! He found the box of chocolate cookies with a thank you note from a contractor at 9:32 and had eaten everything inside of it by 9:51.

Step 2

Attach a wooden floor with a small hole onto the recently assembled wooden 2x4 frame which was just slightly taller than the car and big enough to fit around the car. The key was that it didn't actually touch the car, the last thing they wanted to do was scrape or dent it!

Step 3

Assemble the walls on top of the floor which were held into place loosely with 2 pins per wall. Each pin had a length of rope attached to it which was attached to a longer length of rope run through the receiving door to a hidden compartment in the ceiling where Hunter and Larry had set up a command centre. Some thin cardboard was placed on top as a roof of sorts: people would have been suspicious of an open-air toilet.

Step 4

Place an actual toilet, a returned unit which had been sitting in plumbing for weeks. Gregor had actually yelled at the department head to get it out of the aisle. He would probably be happy his instructions were followed. It was lifted onto the base and screwed into place.

The placement of the drainage hole was critical. They made sure the bottom of the toilet was placed just above the sunroof of the car which was conveniently open because Gregor left the keys with receiving in case a truck came in and they needed to move it (but they were to call him first. Moving it was a last-ditch option if he was in a meeting or on a call.)

Step 5

Make it look like the door to this contraption was a temporary toilet with appropriate signage.

Step 6

Put a sign on the regular toilet stating that it was closed for maintenance.

It was 12:55, done with 5 minutes to spare. Dennis was like clockwork, not as much in his work habits but in his bathroom habits for sure! He usually needed to hit the can at 1:00pm sharp! Consequently, nobody wanted to be near the bathroom for the one o'clock Dennis. There was also a 7:30am, 8:10am, 9am, 11am and 3pm Dennis... that much in meant that much out!

At 12:54 Dennis looked at his watch, he was hungry and felt he was close enough this break to grab a burger... that was until he received what felt like a punch in the gut. For a moment he was shocked, until it felt like someone was pumping air into his guts and overinflating them. He knew he had to go, probably worse than he had ever needed to go before... in his entire life.

Feeling a newfound sense of empathy for women in labour, he gingerly made his way back to the bathroom, his sense of urgency amplified by the massive dose of laxatives he was unaware he had consumed. He arrived at the bathroom in what felt like just in time.

To his utter horror he found a sign directing him to a temporary toilet in receiving: his was out of order!

He moved to receiving as quickly as he could, making sure he took small steps and maintained a narrow, sideways stride. The slightest misstep, hiccup, sneeze, or cough would be catastrophic! He found the new bathroom and didn't even care if it was poorly lit and there was no sink in it, he wasn't much of a hand washer anyway. Dennis had run out of time to think and his strained, cramping muscles could hold back the deluge no longer!

He dropped his drawers and let loose, spilling his percolating guts into that poor toilet. As the pressure subsided, he relaxed and began to look around the temporary bathroom, waiting for the last of the foul gasps from the demon which had possessed his lower intestine. He sat there even longer as he contemplated the lack of toilet paper and how he was going to get out of there.

As that was happening, Gregor was paged back to receiving. Timed perfectly to coincide with when he walked around the corner, Hunter and Larry pulled their rope and the 4 walls of the toilet fell way to reveal Dennis. His pants were around his ankles and Gregor nearly fainted when he saw Dennis sitting on the toilet as it drained into his open sunroof!

Hunter and Larry were there to make Gregor's life hard, not to ruin his stuff. What he didn't see was that they ran a pipe from the toilet into the car and there was a bucket to catch everything. Dennis didn't crap all over Gregor's car, but Gregor didn't know this at the time.

Gregor turned bright red, started shaking and pacing receiving in what could only be described as an agitated manner. Dennis sat there in full view equally upset and began to yell at Gregor to get him some toilet paper! The yelling match which ensued resulted in the cops coming and responding to a domestic disturbance.

Dennis was given a citation for indecent exposure and public defecation. Gregor was given a ticket as his insurance had expired only three days prior. Both were warned not to repeat their behavior. As the cops lectured them, some of the staff looked on while others subtlety hid the evidence of their crime and reconnected the security feed from receiving which had been taken offline earlier that day.

End of the day there were no real consequences. Nobody saw anything and nobody cared. Gregor got his welcome to *their* store and learned that when he wasn't nice to people, people were not nice to him! He drove home that night knowing that they nearly pushed him over the edge that day, he would need to make some changes.

Summer Days

The onset of summer weather in June is a welcome thing for many: it meant a few months of living outside and enjoying the outdoors. For others, it meant weather warm enough to flaunt their body. For Beulla, it was an opportunity to show the men of Retail Depot what they were missing... and in clothes that were far too tight and showed way too much!

Beulla had always had issues understanding how to dress appropriately at work. Every person needs to remember only 1 thing when it comes to fashion: choose clothing that works with your body type, not against it. Not only did her clothing work against her body type, but it was also a crime against humanity! You cannot dress in clothing and outfits meant for women who were 110 pounds when you look like you just ate a woman who was 110 pounds!

On the first warm day of June, she came into work wearing a bright orange mini skirt. It was at least a couple sizes too small and hid zero details of her ass, right down to the growing sweat stains. It had to have been spandex or a super stretchy t-shirt like material because it hugged (more like clung to in valiant protest) what little of her it covered. If you walked in on her bending over in that outfit you might have thought... giant pumpkin that had spoiled, a bag of dead puppies, perhaps new bulk packaging for 15-pound sacks of cottage cheese...

She spent most of the day trying to show off her body to everyone by prefacing it as "This is only for Stephano" and then showing off anyway. On more than one occasion, she heard back that she should have saved it for Stephano.

When one of the part-timers explained to Terry what she was wearing, his wry reply that this was the first time in his life he had ever been grateful for being blind!

By midday she had sweat through that skirt! Her clothes were wet and were starting to smell like onions and ass cheese that had marinated in a bottle of spoiled milk. Even her chair was soaked with sweat in a shroud of Turin-like manner... except that instead of the blood of Jesus it was the sweat of Grimace!

For lunch, she went to the buffet at the casino down the street. Before she left, she loudly proclaimed that she was going there and that she hoped they didn't kick her out because they thought she was a prostitute. Most prostitutes don't head straight to the buffet in a casino and even fewer spend that much time in the washroom after lunch, so she was probably safe!

The food served at the casino was normally good quality: prepared properly and safely. However, on the day she went, there was an issue. Murray was a new line cook who left some fish out on the counter a little too long when he was distracted by something else. Darren took the completed food and covered the tray with foil but didn't put in in the fridge right away as Murray interrupted his work to ask him a few questions. Before it even hit the floor and Neil put in on the steam tray it tasted just a little off. Moreover, it sat out for 10 more minutes while he fiddled with the temperature of the steam table. It sat on the steam table for hours and hours and what was a small issue got worse and worse.

A number of people got sick that day from eating the fish, most had a little nausea or cramping but then again, most only ate a few forkfuls. Beulla loudly exclaimed "mmmm... fish!!!!" when she saw it and ate a whole plate, then ate more in her 6th trip up the buffet!

Several hours later as she sat in her chair, those chubby legs up on the desk exposing the staff to sights and smells they never wanted to know existed, it happened. She turned green. Well not green but the colour definitely drained from her face. She stood up and high-pitched little farts squeaked out as she covered her mouth in shock.

As quickly as she covered her mouth with one hand, she reached behind and under her disgustingly short skirt and attempted to cover her backside. She moved as fast as anyone had ever seen her move, albeit awkwardly, and made her way to the bathroom. They didn't see or hear her for hours but Roz from special services had tried to go pee on her way back from her break. She had heard and smelled what Beulla had been up to and quickly left the area! Roz had older brothers and knew full well the dangers of woft.

As she described it, imagine the sound of an off-key baritone sax being played under water combined with the agonized cries of a dying hippo. When she went into the bathroom it was sort of quiet and just as she tried to go, someone or something went very wrong in the handicap stall.

She heard Beulla's voice and a childlike whimper saying "uh oh... oh no... mmmmmmm... oh no... ahhhhhhhhh... nnnnnnnnnn... ahhhhh-hhhh... oh no!" and then heard sounds she didn't believe a human could make. If it wasn't for the horrid smell, she might have thought the woman in one of the other stalls was having a baby: possibly triplets.

Spirit On the Water

Rosoff was enjoying somewhat of a renaissance at Retail Depot. His tenure at the store did not start out as particularly promising. He had alienated so many people and had become known as the empty vest. However, all of that changed when Gregor took over and gave him a fresh start. Gregor didn't care about what other people thought, he cared that Stephano Rosoff was saying all of the right things and buying into his way of doing things!

Stephano and Ned were Gregor's type of associates: loyal, coachable, mindless yes-men! They became his model associates and their ability to influence things at Retail Depot became a problem. Stephano was finally getting the respect he felt he deserved since the day he started. The people at work who should have been respecting him had not been and he was considering how to make them pay for that now that he was in a position to do so!

From what Stephano saw, Gregor appeared to be onto Hunter and Larry which was one of the reasons he was finally getting the respect he deserved. They were not able to push him around anymore and when they did, he was able to get Gregor up to speed from his side of things first. He still didn't know how they did half the stuff they got away with: it was like they were able to disappear and reappear out of thin air!

Life was finally starting to go Stephano's way. He had also entered into a relationship with another associate who was smart and capable but didn't get all of the respect that she deserved either. He was enjoying his relationship with Beulla who dressed sexily for him and allowed him to achieve his goal of finding a woman who would have sex with him. He had low standards, but they had a lot in common and were even learning to speak Klingon together!

Sitting On a Barbed Wire Fence

ennis was not having such a hot summer. His pro captain combo had made the news (it felt like CBC was sending a crew to the store monthly) and a guy on TV who travelled around and ate at "over the top" restaurants in the US had even come to Winnipeg and did a profile of the combo for his show!

CBC had tried to interview him (Larry and Hunter had been kind enough to point him out once they had given their explanation for the combo) and he tried to run (walked fast, it was Dennis after all) out of the store with a jacket over his head to hide his identity. His face was covered but so were his eyes and he managed to speed walk into a metal support column in his haste. Walked right into it at full speed, hit his head and fell flat on his ass.

He was knocked out momentarily and woke up confused and hungry but proceeded to have both the most honest and hilarious conversation of his life in his concussed state. Best part was that it was all captured on video!

His relationship with Edith was close to over too. He had wanted out for some time: other than the food he was not happy. As it turned out, she felt the same way. It was complicated though, she was worried about being alone and Dennis was loved by her father, Harry. When she told her father it was over, he was sad. It was an emotional discussion with him but when she explained why she was leaving him and that she deserved to be happy, her father did the right thing and supported her.

When the day finally came, they went for breakfast at a local greasy spoon. After eating their meals and several additional orders of pancakes, they decided to end it then rather than trying to hang on for the summer.

After, she walked into Harry's to begin her day as she always did, life went on.

Dennis got in his car and drove to a local sub shop. He too would have to move on and that would mean new ways to pass the time besides hanging out at Harry's. He could have worked harder at Retail Depot, but eating was more fun! It was going to be difficult to find a new favourite restaurant, but he was willing to do the legwork to make the right decision.

Series Of Dreams

Dennis's partnership with Rosoff had also begun to show signs of weakness. It started innocently enough, with Dennis trying to talk Rosoff out of going to Harry's for lunch and coming with him to Burger Guy instead. Neither was good at being wrong and both were even worse at being right. For the stupidest of reasons, a simple discussion turned into a disagreement which got heated!

There was tension at the desk for days, with Stephano purposely bringing combos from Harry's to eat at the desk to in an attempt to torture Dennis. It was hard on him; he simply couldn't bring himself to eat there any longer. He tried at a different location but all he could taste was gravy and heartbreak! He wanted that food but couldn't go back there.

Dennis tried to counter by bringing back food from Burger Guy and eating it at the desk but on the 5-minute drive back he ate most of the food, leaving him with a few cold fries, his 4th and final cheeseburger plus half his milkshake to gloat about.

Stephano's stock was picking up in the store, he was even being considered for Ned's role with Ned moving up to acting assistant manager. His ego was doing a great job compensating for the positive changes at work and he decided to shed the title of assistant to the pro captain. Upon Beulla's urging he decided that he and Dennis would work as equals until his official promotion came through.

Dennis was not enjoying the changes in Stephano. Suddenly Dennis had to pick orders and do work as well. Stephano was no longer listening to him; he had even told Dennis to do something himself. Until that point Dennis was happy with his role as a leader and manager: letting Stephano delegate orders and (only where necessary) do the required heavy lifting. Never had picking his own orders been on the table, until then.

Dennis had a large order for 24 five-gallon buckets of white primer and asked Stephano to pull down the skid for him to which Stephano said "no".

Trying to find someone in operations didn't fix the situation and the pro captain was not successful. Nobody liked him or Rosoff and nobody answered their pages anymore. Ironically Larry did call back when Dennis paged for someone to help him but Dennis curtly said "go to hell" and that he didn't need his help.

Dennis thought it was only the 1 skid and he could easily pull it down himself, so he jumped on one of the big fork-trucks from lumber and proceeded to try to drive it down the aisle. He could have walked across the store and grabbed a smaller forklift from receiving, meant for the narrower aisles but it was a big store, and he didn't feel like walking that far.

He got it to paint easily enough but when he got there, he realized that the forklift he brought was too big for the paint aisle. He really didn't feel like driving that one back to lumber and then walking all the way back to receiving to get one of the smaller lifts for the aisles, so he decided to make it work. Being a leader meant being decisive!

He thought that if he drove in on an angle and then got his forks partly underneath the skid and tilted them up slightly, that he would be able to pull the skid off the shelf. He tried to do it as he had planned and was able to get into the aisle sideways and under the skid.

He went to tilt the skid up and then slowly started to back out of the aisle. He had a very heavy load and a skid that was only partially supported. The weight of half the skid was way too much for the other half and the wooden skid creaked and snapped, completely coming apart. 24 five-gallon pails of primer fell to the ground and exploded! The explosion created a wave of white primer that soaked everyone and everything in the immediate vicinity.

He got off the forklift and proclaimed that the skid was defective and the people who put it up there in the first place should be fired. Then he went to the department head of paint and said he had a customer coming shortly and needed to get ready for his meeting. With that, the weasel skulked away.

The mess took days to clean up, primer sticks to everything! It cost the store a fortune in cleanup costs, lost revenue, and labour. Despite a very long clean-up, it only took about 15 minutes for Gregor to figure out what happened. He would have to discuss with head office and HR before he could make any decision. Legal and HR would need to be consulted above store level.

Everyone in the store knew what was coming next. Dennis was sent home and told to come in at 9am, not his normal start time of 7am. After making the lives of everyone in the store miserable, it looked like the illustrious reign of the pro captain was coming to an end!

That night Hunter and Larry discussed it over drinks with some of the other associates. One of them raised an important issue: how would they properly send off their nemesis the pro captain?

Hunter proposed that they send him off with a song, but what song? It was Larry who suggested they write their own. Mack and Mr. Chill were there so they had musicians to assist them but what kind of song would it be?

Hunter was the one who started it as a joke, but they all worked until late into the night to finish it. They went back to Chill's basement studio and asked Mack to sing it to American Pie so they could record it.

A long long time ago
I can still remember how
the line-up at Harry's was long
and at the front we found our Dennis
A bacon double cheese with a poutine,
onion rings and ice cream sandwiches please

But the ax fell down pushed by Gregor
In a moment our pro captain was gone
no lazy man to avoid work
no endless hours on a break

I can't remember when he worked hard
none of us remember him being that smart
but he never hurt a soul, oh no
why did he have to go?
Go?

Bye, bye Mr. burgers and fries
Drove my Chevy to the Harry's but the fryer was dry
And them good ole boys weren't having burgers with extra cheese
Singin' we won't have a heart attack and die
no we won't have a heart attack and die

Starting when you punched in for your shift
Why did you take some many breaks
Yes you were hungry we know.
Couldn't you wait a bit more?
you were not terrible but you weren't a saint
what were you thinking doing that in paint?

Bye, bye Mr. burgers and fries
Drove my Chevy to the Harry's but the fryer was dry
And them good ole boys weren't having burgers with extra cheese
Singin' we won't have a heart attack and die
no we won't have a heart attack and die

I met a man, his name was Roosif
And as it turned out he was useless
He hung his pro captain out to dry

It was his weakest excuse yet
receiving having needed to be swept
so the man had to pull the paint himself instead

And in the aisles and on the ground
nearly killed by the wave of paint that washed around

the floors there will be white for life
The staff couldn't clean it before it dried

Bye, bye Mr. burgers and fries
Drove my Chevy to the Harry's but the fryer was dry
And them good ole boys weren't having burgers with extra cheese
Singin' we won't have a heart attack and die
no we won't have a heart attack and die

They were singing
Bye, bye Mr. burgers and fries
Drove my Chevy to the Harry's but the fryer was dry
And them good ole boys weren't having burgers with extra cheese
Singin' we won't have a heart attack and die
no we won't have a heart attack and die

The song was recorded that night and as Dennis was being led out of the store at 9:05am the next morning, Larry played it through his excessively loud car stereo. For days after people were humming it and singing it… "bye bye Mr. burgers and fries"!

The saga of the pro captain was over. They had outlasted him, and, in the end, he had brought about his own demise, and it had nothing to do with them. The same part of his personality which had made him so difficult to work with also caused his undoing. He would be missed only for his comedic value.

Romance In Durango

Things move fast in life and in love. After getting engaged, Donny decided that he didn't want to wait and set a date for the end of the summer. To pay for the wedding, he held a Stag and Doe party.

The Stag and Doe was one of the greatest summer traditions of all time. For $30 you got all you could eat (usually roast pig, BBQ chicken and burgers) and all of the beer you could keep down. They were always animated events and would usually raise enough money to fund the wedding.

The unofficial all-hands parties happened about once a month and, on most occasions, everyone who attended was an equal no matter what their job title was at work. This one was different because for the first time in a very long time, the store manager did not attend. Gregor didn't think it was professional to hang out with his staff outside of work and let it be known to all of the assistant managers that he felt this applied to them too.

Only one of the assistant managers did show up: in fact, it was held at his house. Jamie knew that his career and his time at Retail Depot was winding down. He had thrived under Kenneth but had no success with Gregor and, from conversations with other stores, he knew that Gregor liked a project to focus on and he was that project. Since he was going to be leaving anyway, he decided to spend what little time he had left with the people he cared about.

The house was rocking! His large, now partially finished basement held the band and the dance floor. The kitchen held the bar and some of the staff went and once again hot-boxed his double garage, this time he sat in the middle of the circle and held court!

Hunter was celebrating 1 year at Retail Depot and for the first time felt like he belonged someplace. In such a short period of time, these people had become like family, and he loved working with them. He had friends all around him by then, had pretty much decided not to return to school. He knew there were other careers which were better paying, had better hours, titles, etc. but he doubted that he would ever find another group of people like that again and it was not lost on him.

He hadn't intended to grow up but along the way, but all of the people he worked with had rubbed off a little on him. He was young and brash when he joined the staff at the store. He still played a few too many pranks (perhaps having a little too much fun at work) but had become known as a solid guy. Dennis's assessment of him as a spoiled rich kid might have stuck had he not proven it wrong day in and day out.

He looked around and saw his friends and colleagues. He saw people who worked hard every day and didn't complain about it. He saw a woman he had serious feelings for over in the corner talking to her friends. He took it all in. Maybe it was the moment or maybe it was too much time in the garage, but he felt a welling up of pride. He decided then and there to stay at Retail Depot in one of those life-defining moments!

After midnight as the party started to wind down a group of people decided to drive 45 minutes to a local beach and keep the party going under the stars. They parked on the beach and climbed the lighthouse tower to finish the night in a more relaxed and scenic manner.

A joint followed the conversation, moving in a circular manner and arriving on the topic of the future. Several people asked Hunter what his plans were in the fall. Hunter casually explained that he was not going back to school and that he was happy where he was.

A few of the people there got very mad at him. Most of them didn't have a chance to get an education: they were simply trying to find the best job they could get in life and get the most out of work that they could. They were upset that he was throwing away the opportunity they never had. He may not have been the most well-loved associate when he started but they loved him then and they wanted him to have more out of life than they had. If he were to succeed, it would be like he took them all with him. If he failed, they all would all fail too.

Larry, in his very inebriated state, put it best. "We would hate to lose you: you are my best friend! At the same time, we would hate it more if you blew the opportunity to do this. I would love to, but I know I won't be able to, you can! Do it and make us all proud!"

Hunter knew he needed to do something: he wouldn't be able to hide behind his vest forever, but he didn't know what to do yet. He didn't want to leave those people or that life behind, it was not easy to find happiness and even harder to let it go once you had a taste of it.

He looked around. His best friend, his girlfriend and some of the most virtuous and upright people he had ever known were sitting beside him. It may have been just a job in the beginning, but it was much more than a job by then.

For the drive home in the morning, he sat in silence. His girlfriend was asleep on the seat beside him. Larry and his girlfriend in the backseat, also passed out. He had started the night firmly committed to staying at Retail Depot and forgetting about school. Yet all his friends wanted him to finish, to make more of himself than he could just by working. He was torn and didn't know what to do: he just wanted to make sure that he did the right thing!

Pressing On

For several months Rosoff and Beulla appeared to have the perfect relationship. They seemed happy and it kept both of them busy enough not to bother everyone else as much. The problem with work relationships is that they overlap at work and while Rosoff agreed with Beulla that she needed a leadership role, he could not force Gregor to see it too.

One evening they were hanging out in his apartment (his apartment was actually his parents old 34-foot Triple E motorhome which he kept parked on a secluded corner of their 60-acre property, it would have been nice had it still been 1981) and she was pressing him on the subject. He mostly wanted to get busy and fall asleep. He was not a long-term thinker and decided to agree to help her once and for all so she would have sex with him. His plan worked, he had seven of the hottest (and sweatiest) minutes of his entire life and they both passed out and fell asleep.

The next day he thought that it was just talk but she did not: she was very serious! Stephano spent most of the following week pleading his case for her to join the management program. He explained that she is a talker yes, but also very capable and a natural leader if given some respect! He explained this to anyone who would listen but with zero success.

His last attempt came when he tried to position her as the natural successor to the assistant of the recently departed pro captain. It was not to be though: Gregor had decided to cancel the program in his store since sales to contractors had actually increased after Dennis left. Rosoff was not going to be named his successor either. Gregor had already decided not to replace Dennis: contractors could deal directly with the departments as they needed to. Rosoff would delegate the picking of orders but very little else and would return to ops until a new role opened up for him.

That night as Beulla and Stephano drank their wine cocktails (take a glass, add cheap wine, ice cubes and apple juice) he explained that there was no role for her. She got very upset. "But you promised!"

He had promised her and he had failed. The truth was that he never had any power to make that promise and he just wanted to get laid, but she didn't care. She expected very little of her man, made obvious by the fact that she was dating him, but she did expect honesty. She did really care about him, but she knew that she couldn't let him walk all over her, so for the very first time in her life, she actually stood up for herself.

"You know what Stephano? I don't mind that you work all of the time and are married to your career, and I love being with you, but I am not sure I can stay with a man who lies to me! If you cannot help me, make it to management that's ok but you should have said so: instead, you got me all worked up and then broke my heart. I do not know if we can go on like this together."

They talked for several hours and decided to take a break from each other to sort themselves out.

On Wednesday when Rosoff came into work, he came with a chip on his shoulder. He was out of the best (and only) relationship he had ever been in because none of the other managers would give his girl a chance. He had to deal with managers who lacked vision and he was surrounded by people who were not worthy of walking beside him. To top it all off, he was pretty sure that he heard Hunter page him as Roosif (He had been paged as Stephano Rosoff, but it sounded like Roosif because he only heard part of it.)!

He marched into the phone centre to confront him. It had been a rough week and he had heard enough. He didn't walk in quietly; he violently pushed the door in and made a lot of noise doing it. "You are so done buddy; you know you can't call me Roosif anymore and everyone just heard it! Buh bye you college jackass!"

Hunter denied it. Terry denied he had said it and several other associates swore that he paged him properly, which he had. Beulla didn't hear any of the page: she was on the phone at the time. As mad as she was at Stephano, she hated Hunter more and how they always picked on Stephano. "I heard him do it! I heard him say Watch this" I am going to page Roosif and he did!"

Stephano smiled. He knew that their brief separation was over, she took his side, and he was finally going to get rid of Hunter. The only problem was that they were the only 2 who had heard the page: everyone else heard the correct page including Gregor. After raising the issue with him, Gregor told him to back down and quit trying to set the kid up. Gregor would deal with him when the time was right.

Rosoff was angry. When Ned arrived for his closing shift later and was briefed, he too was upset. They were tired of waiting for upper management to see things from their point of view and instead decided to declare war on Hunter, Larry and everyone else who dared cross them. They had an ally in Beulla and because pretty much everything that happened in the store went through the phone centre, she would be able to help him with their plan.

They spent several weeks enforcing small petty rules, trying to write people up for doing things that they themselves had only recently done. They clocked break times, reported violations of company dress code and even gave warnings to associates who did not strictly adhere to the dreaded 5-foot rule* and desperately searching for the person who kept paging that stupid cow sound!

*The 5-foot rule meant that if an associate was not with another customer, they had to say hello to every customer within 5 feet and offer to help them. Great idea if you worked in flooring and a customer was in flooring but nearly impossible to get things done if you were trying to get across the store or put product away

Their newfound power had been exactly what Ned and Stephano wanted but how they wielded it had managed to rub pretty much everyone the wrong way. Making matters worse, Beulla had begun to feel important too and now was able to enlist her sometimes boyfriend to help enforce her decrees. "Either you do what I am telling you or I will page Stephano and he and Ned will make you do it!" It made for a lot of tension and discomfort at work.

Eventually, Hunter could take no more. After hearing Beulla tell a part timer that he had to do what she said or she would get Stephano to fire him, he decided to deal with the issue once and for all.

He still had the number of the president of Retail Depot, and he decided to use it. He called her and explained that he would be leaving the company because a few associates were bullying the rest of the associates and it had become too stressful to work there. She was delighted to hear from him but saddened to hear that he would be leaving (he wasn't planning to). Sounding truly empathetic he lamented it was too bad that 3 people had managed to poison an entire store and it's too bad they couldn't get a fresh start where they could be judged on their merits and not on their histories and baggage.

She thought his suggestion was a wonderful idea and would make it happen if he agreed not to quit, which he did.

In the morning, he showed up for work with a smile on his face. Some of the other associates asked what the big "shit-eating" grin was all about, and he told them to wait! Starting at 9am, one by one, Ned and then Stephano and then Beulla were called into the manager's office for 30 minutes each and all left the store as soon as their meeting ended. Knowing at least 1 of them could not get fired, the staff were not sure what was going on.

The next morning, at the staff meeting before the store opened and again at the afternoon staff meeting, everyone heard why they had left. All three had been transferred to the new concept store which Retail Depot was opening in Alaska. Ned would go as a full assistant manager; Stephano would assume the role of pro captain and Beulla would finally be the captain of a phone centre. All it cost them was everything they knew in the town they grew up in and taking a post at the end of the earth!

When someone leaves, you are supposed to congratulate them and had the three of them been even remotely decent people, there might have been a party held in their honour and a vest signed by everybody. Instead, everyone cheered loudly and openly. They were going to be leaving and going so far away that it would take several flights to get back. It was going to be a place of extreme cold and isolation and if ever there was such a thing as justice, surely this was it.

Beulla was floating, having just received a promotion even if there was no formal change in title, salary or responsibility. The move would turn out to be very good for her though. Half of her problem was that she lived at home with 2 parents who may or may not have been cousins.

Ned was excited too, having finally broken through the glass ceiling and taken his 'rightful' place in upper management. He didn't really like the snow but thought it would be fun to live an outdoor lifestyle and he had his dog to take with him. It was a 4 or 5 day drive: he hoped his dog didn't get the farts again!

Stephano didn't know what to think. He felt like he was being banished to a far kingdom instead of the palace his family had built. He also felt like someone as important as he should be in a more prominent location and not a smaller expansion store in the middle of nowhere. He did have Beulla going there with him, so all was not lost: he looked over at her sitting at a table in the lunchroom… those massive legs barely covered by that stretched skirt… the way her cheeks turned red when she passed wind or after sex… he was one lucky man!

He tried to make the best of it and throw it back in Hunter's face. Hunter was pretty quick to ask him why he was going to Alaska and who he thought had made the call which got him sent into exile. Hunter had to explain it to him a few times before he understood how and who. It took a while, but he finally realized what had actually transpired!

All the colour drained from his face. He knew that Hunter was not lying. Hunter said it was the best way to get rid of him: sending him to the edge of the empire where he could enjoy the arctic cold, long nights with no daylight and listening to Beulla talk to him all night long as the northern lights played overhead.

Roosif said nothing but in his head, he heard James T. Kirk yelling Kahhhhhhhhhnnnnnnn!

Political World

The Roosif had been beaten. He knew it and finally realized it. He looked like he was about to yell at Hunter but instead just walked away. Hunter stood there. Victory felt good but hollow and empty at the same time: he had lost his greatest opponent. He wanted to leave Rosoff alone and just let it be, but the man known as Roosif had different plans.

He and Ned were upset when they realized that their transfer had come directly from the president, why it occurred and knowing they had no ability to change her mind. Instead, they decided to turn the tables on Hunter and Larry by trying to feed them some of their own medicine.

They did try everything they could think of in their 2 weeks left in town. They also tried replying to various adult personal ads to create an embarrassing situation for them but had no luck in convincing someone to show up at the store to meet. They tried calling HR and the tip line at HQ to report Hunter for theft, fraud and selling company secrets but without proof they just looked petty.

Rosoff's last attempt to settle the score was his worst yet. Ned had been on it initially but had walked away after several previous unsuccessful tries had made him look even more petty!

Hunter spent very little time discussing his situation at school and even less showing off up his bowling abilities. He purposely didn't sign up for the store bowling team (which broke Uncle Dale's heart) in the local league just to stay under the radar. He had gone from being a kid who referred to himself as a student and bowler, to just being himself and that he worked in the phone centre at Retail Depot.

In the morning Hunter walked in to begin his shift as he always did. He walked to the back of the store to don his vest before punching in. When he walked into the lunchroom where the punch clock was, he was greeted by a copy of the cover of Sports Illustrated he had been featured on. It felt like so long ago and when he saw it, he knew that he was nothing like the smug kid in the picture, so it was no big deal. It had been copied and placed all over his locker and the rest of the lunchroom. When he got to his locker, he found it sealed tightly with glue and the lock wrapped in shrink wrap.

Rosoff was sitting down enjoying his fries and gravy, basking in the perceived glory of his accomplishment. He had <u>shown</u> Hunter what happens when you messed with him. He remembered all of the times he had blown up at Hunter when he had played all of those stupid pranks on him: he was getting ready for the explosion. He knew that in the public of the lunchroom he would lose his temper and erupt and then everyone would see him for who he really was.

Instead, he saw Hunter walk in and notice all of his work and start to laugh exclaiming "That's great!" while looking at him and smiling. He didn't even react to the locker. Rosoff had expected him to get mad or at least try to open the locker but instead he walked to where the new vests were, simply put one on and punched in.

Stephano was expecting something he didn't get and finally decided to do something a little more rash...

He walked back to the manager's office and called the police, reporting that Hunter was a recently terminated associate who had returned to the store. He was stealing and was suspected of selling drugs, having been asked to leave the store. When asked his name he gave Dennis's name and smiled at his own cleverness.

What he didn't know was that Dennis was actually at the police station as the call was being made. He wasn't being arrested: he had gotten a job with the city to maintain the police station and was changing out some exit signs. He was already well known there as he was written up three times for eating all of the donuts in the lunchroom. Three times! On his first, second and third days at work.

Luckily the office manager had some experience raising both hogs and teenage boys as well as dealing with donut hungry cops. She was able to deal with it. On day number four she started ordering way more donuts and by day eight Dennis had eaten so many that he was temporarily sick of them.

So, when the call came in, the woman in dispatch was curious as to how the man who kept eating all of their donuts and who was currently changing a sign across the hallway, could be calling from a store he no longer worked at.

She decided to send a car down to the store to find some answers. Either they would arrest someone for dealing drugs and theft or they would find the person who had wasted their time.

The officer who arrived was one Constable Scott and he was nearly 7 feet tall. He towered over everyone and spent a few moments speaking to Joseph who assured him that while Hunter was a pain in the ass, he was not a drug dealer. He still asked to speak to Hunter and asked to see his locker.

When they got to the lunchroom, Rosoff was there on yet another break and watched with delight as Hunter was asked to open his locker. Hunter pointed to his locker and explained that he would love to but (pointing to Rosoff) "that ball of grease" glued it shut and taped his lock.

Rosoff vehemently denied it but 6 or 7 people stood up and said that they saw him do it. He was quickly forced to explain that it was just a prank and a joke between friends. Constable Scott asked him if he might have any idea who called the cops on Hunter because while some childish prank on a locker is perhaps mischief, falsifying a police report is a very serious offence that could yield some very serious consequences.

Hunter saw the cop staring at Rosoff and saw Rosoff nervously looking back at him. "Officer, I don't want to press charges. He is about to undertake a huge move to Alaska and see that thing in the short skirt walking in (pointing at Beulla as Rosoff yelled out 'HEY!')? He has that to go home to every night, I don't want to get in the way of any of those things… the guy has enough problems!"

The cop made a face as though someone was holding a small turd under his nose when he looked at her. From that bob of brassy red hair to the uncovered midriff dripping over the waist band of a skirt several sizes too small and 6 inches too short, she was dripping sexuality and large amounts of sweat. He knew that Rosoff had a lot of problems and decided that it was not worth the investigation: he had no desire to interview him or to meet her!

The cop apologized to Hunter and shook his hand, leaving the store to find a real crime. The only crime he could see there was Beulla's outfit.

Hunter calmly walked up to Rosoff and said "I know it was you Fredo" and kissed him on the cheek. The staff in the lunchroom burst out laughing. Rosoff had tried to compete, and he hadn't even come close. The sun was setting on his time in the store, and it was to the sound of laughter.

Hunter left the room and Rosoff was left trying to figure out what went wrong. As Beulla quietly broke wind while trying to console him, he realized was starting to feel ok about leaving. It's tough working someplace where everyone else was an idiot and most other people were wrong all of the time.

The following week the 3 of them were given a week off to fly up and try to find a place to live. Rosoff and Beulla found a nice apartment and set up shop. It was small but they made it work by being smart: taking the dishes into the bath with them, bathing and washing their laundry minimally and by making large pots of chili each week which caused gas but created endless cheap entertainment.

Ned ended up finding a room in a house with a single woman in her 50's and a couple of other bachelors just like him. It turned out that the lady he was renting from was quite into S&M, a dominatrix, and the other men were her slaves. He didn't see it coming but over time they wore him down and within a month he was quite happy spending his time in a black leather mask doing what he was told! Some of the things he used to laugh about and tease other people for turned out to be his favourite things in Alaska!

Pay In Blood

enry was as hardworking of a man as you would ever hope to meet. He took care of his family and several other families: they relied on him for everything. He worked hard at his job because of his ethic and because so many people were depending on him for so much. He was one of those guys who was always helping others too.

On a quiet Tuesday night, he was finishing his shift when someone paged for a lift truck driver to help pull down a tub on a skid for a waiting customer. He had already punched out, but it was just a single skid and he took down dozens every day. Not wanting to keep a customer waiting, he made his way over to plumbing where Hunter was waiting for him. It was a phone sale to an out-of-town customer and Hunter was just trying to take care of the customer.

He jumped on the truck and Hunter sent the young part timer from ops over to the other aisle to spot while he spotted for Henry in the working aisle. Henry started to inch up to the skid and get his forks in. What he did not know was that a piece of the skid was broken and by lifting it up, the skid had dangled down and was caught in front of the support shelving for that 8-foot section. Henry tried to turn the skid to dislodge it but instead the dangling piece of 2x4 was hooked on the shelving unit.

The shelving was anchored to the cement floors below, so it did not come off the ground at first but as he pulled back harder to get loose, it was enough force to pull it away from its base and sheer the aged bolts right off.

The skid finally came free but so did the shelving unit and as he saw the shelf start to tilt toward him, he powered forward and the normally solid shelf fell forward too. It came down with a crash into the next shelf which set up a cascading effect and brought down 3 more sets of shelving in a massive pile-up of metal, concrete and 6 figures worth of merchandise.

Henry slid off the lift: a look of horror on his face. This sort of accident was not acceptable to a professional like him and was made even worse because he was off the clock when it happened. He knew what would happen and that finding work for a guy in his late 50's was no easy feat in the current economy.

Hunter checked to see if he was ok first and then told him to say nothing: that he would handle it. Gregor and the rest of the managers came running to the scene and demanded to know what happened and if everyone was alright. Hunter stepped up and told Gregor that he was driving the lift at the time, and it was his fault. Gregor told him to go wait in the office and started to talk to other people.

Henry walked up to him in the office while he was waiting and asked him why he had said it was his fault. Hunter replied that he only had to take care of himself, and he was sure not going to let him get fired for trying to help him when nobody else would.

Henry protested citing that Hunter didn't have his licence and would get fired to which Hunter simply responded "Someone is probably going to get fired… I can find another job more easily than you can".

Gregor came into the office with Uncle Dale and Joseph and asked him to fill out and sign several reports and forms. Then they asked him again about the accident. There was no camera in that area but several people in the vicinity said it was Henry who drove the truck, not Hunter. They had asked Henry if he saw anything and he had said that it was his fault, not Hunter's. Hunter simply said Henry was trying to help him out, but he got frustrated and impatient and tried to pull the tub down himself.

They gave Hunter one more shot to explain what happened and he just repeated himself, so they told him that he needed to show up at the store at 9am on Friday and he knew what that meant. He knew he was done but hopefully it had saved Henry his job and helped him make it those last 2 years until he qualified for his pension.

When Friday came around, Hunter showed up as instructed. As he awaited his fate, he saw Henry who came over to him and told him to quit lying for him to save his ass, that he had already admitted to it. Hunter asked what they were going to do to him. Henry explained he was going to be severely written up but would be allowed to continue working. HR said it was only because they couldn't prove that it was him and with 2 people admitting to it, it would be a difficult lawsuit to defend.

Henry told him that he had saved his job and now Hunter needed to save his own job by telling the truth. Hunter knew that if he did that Henry would be fired and he would probably still be fired. By then he had filed official documents and statements. There was no going back, only forward.

As he walked into the office, he was surprised to see 2 people he had not seen in a very long time. His father and his university bowling coach were both in the office and for a moment Hunter thought it was some sort of bizarre intervention. Gregor asked him to sit down and said that before he dealt with the incident at work there were some people who needed to share a few things.

He explained that a number of the managers and staff had asked him to call the coach to tell him that Hunter was not the same person he was when he first arrived at Retail Depot. The coach heard about how he had risen to some serious challenges and had helped out so many other people, including Henry. The legendary bowling coach said he was impressed and that no matter what happened in that office, he would like to welcome him back to the school and the team in the fall.

His father echoed the same sentiment and expressed his pride in his son and shared a letter that Ralph of all people had written to him. Hunter's dad had never heard people say good things about his son and it seemed to him that his time at Retail Depot was time well spent.

No matter what happened at work, his father and his coach got a chance to see and hear about the type of person he had become. He had earned a spot back on the bowling team and would be able to resume his education. Except, he didn't want to do that anymore.

He explained that he wanted to work at Retail Depot and liked his life there. Gregor told him it was not that easy and that he had no choice given the circumstances. He protested but Gregor was right: he had admitted to driving a lift without a licence and taken the blame for a major accident in the process. It was devastating but he knew how much Henry's family would have lost and he was glad to have been able to help them.

He stood up and shook everyone's hand and prepared to be led out of the store, away from people who had become like family to him, away from his friends. He closed his eyes, breathed in deeply and got ready to walk out of the store one last time: preparing as best he could for his turn doing his walk of shame.

As he emerged from the receiving doors flanked by his managers, his coach and his father he was greeted by something he had never expected to see. There, lining the main aisle was nearly every associate from the store. As he slowly walked down that aisle he hugged them, shook their hands and started to well up.

He was being led away from people he loved and a place he truly enjoyed being a part of. At the end of the aisle by the exit doors was Mr. Chill, Mack, Terry, Ralph, Larry and Sarita: all of his closest friends. He was overwhelmed and he was not the only one who was crying. It was Ralph who was bawling the most and simply said "I am gonna miss you, you crazy bastard!"

As he prepared to walk out the door one last time, he heard applause as he people he had spent the last 14 months with saluted him. He also heard the sound of dozens of cows mooing. All of his friends had bought the same noisemakers to salute him and see him off in the best way they could.

As he walked towards his car, he saw the words "In Roosif we Trust" woven between the links of the fence in the parking lot in that thin, half ply toilet paper that was supplied in the store bathrooms.

It was over as it began: in the parking lot of the Retail Depot.

He got in his car and drove away, knowing it would be for the last time. Eyes welling again, tears falling but his held was held high. He was sad but he knew he did the right thing, even if the right thing was a difficult sacrifice.

What began as a job to fill time became much, much more. There he learned what it meant to be a decent person, the value of true friendship, that a person is not defined by their income or title and that being a solid person meant doing what was right. His pay was merely monetary, but his reward was the kind of growth that leads to endless acts of kindness and a lifetime of happiness.

Epilogue

Hunter returned to school in the fall and unlike last time, he had a very different and much more mature attitude. He was a better student, a better bowler and spent his time with better people. He was a better person!

This time he didn't just hang around with his beer buddies going to parties and wasting time: he worked hard and he played hard. He spent time with his friends from Retail Depot every week and often skipped parties on campus, electing for the Saturday night parties with them instead. He didn't work there anymore but he stayed very close to his retail family.

He started to spend more time with his real family too, having finally earned his father's respect.

At the end of his first semester back he was approached by a marketing company from New York who had tracked him down. The entire Roosif campaign had not gone unnoticed, and the marketing guys wanted to know if he would licence the name, as a major chain store (not named) Retail Depot wanted to use it for an international campaign.

He said he would licence it but with just one condition, that his partner Larry also get credit for it and instead of Hunter getting money, Larry would get to go to school and get an education too. He had a shot at an education because of good fortune in a bowling alley one night, Larry deserved a similar opportunity. The marketing company happily agreed, they were prepared to pay a lot of money for the name. There were pleasantly surprised when all Hunter wanted was for a guy he used to work with to go to school for 3 years!

The Years After!

Over the years many of the people in this story left the Retail Depot. Some took other jobs or went to other locations. A few retired and a few were let go. Sadly, a few passed away as well.

However, a great many of them stayed there and kept going. Almost a decade after Hunter and Larry's time there, the decision was made to demolish the store and build a newer and larger one elsewhere in town. As the store was being demolished the tunnels and secret room were discovered. Many of their things still there, including their famous logbook of mischief.

The staff were asked about it and there was a great deal of laughter. A number of people said "That's how they did it!" and while both had long since moved out of town, they remained legends. Even new hires were aware of their exploits. The new store was nicer and cleaner but lacked the multiple carvings of a bloated rat which had given the old location some of its character.

Hunter
Hunter would go on to win two more national titles bowling with U of W, a record unrivaled by any other college bowler. He went on to a short but spectacular career in professional bowling, retiring at the age of

twenty-eight as one of the winningest bowlers of all time and he made good deal of money doing it.

Having spent his spare time working on an MBA, Hunter graduated towards the end of his bowling career and started several small technology and retail security companies, one of which got very big and was ironically purchased by Retail Depot. Twelve years after being escorted out of one of their stores, he was back. He had the title of chief technology officer with a big office in their HQ in Maine.

He stayed with Sarita and three summers after he left Retail Depot, they were married with many of their friends from Retail Depot present. They have been very happily married since. Larry threw a bachelor party which was one for the ages and in recounting some of their exploits at work, gave one of the funniest wedding speeches of all time! They have two small children, a dog and a bowling alley in their basement.

Larry

Larry never expected to go to college but took the opportunity that the marketing company from New York offered him. He spent two full years at U of W with Hunter as they both enjoyed student life and remained very close friends on campus. After Hunter graduated, Larry transferred to a school in New York City and finished his degree with honours. After he finished school, he also got married: Hunter was his best man.

He worked in marketing and became very successful, creating a life that he could have never imagined for himself: so much so that he was also hired back by the Retail Depot. He had gone from pulling orders and dealing with lazy colleagues to a senior manager of marketing and branding. His office was just down the hall from Hunter's and by all accounts, they still push boundaries, even in their senior roles. None of the other executives still have any idea who keeps interrupting their meetings…

Rosoff

Rosoff only lasted 1 year in Alaska. He and Beulla did not last more than 5 months, and she left him and returned to her family. He knew that he was going to go no further in Retail Depot and opted to leave in search of a better opportunity. He found work in an oil patch in northern Alberta and found a job that was perfect for his skills, abilities and work ethic. He worked in receiving at a remote facility and spent a great deal of his time sitting around, waiting for trucks and, you guessed it, sweeping receiving.

He thought he had left the curse of Roosif behind but was extremely upset to see that the foreman at the camp loved the sketch on SNL and had a picture of Dana Carvey dressed in his Roosif outfit in the main hallway, meaning he had to walk right past a Roosif every day!

Ned

Ned actually thrived in Alaska for a while and enjoyed the balance between his job, at which he was doing well and his hobby of S&M. After several years of service, he felt that he needed a change and decided to move to LA to live the life twenty-four seven and the last anybody heard he was working in the adult film industry. Some swore he was doing fetish movies: others that he was recording autoerotic asphyxiation videos. He wears a collar and spends much of his spare time in a basement dungeon in LA.

Beulla

Her time in Alaska away from everyone and everything she knew proved to be very valuable for her and fostered some much-needed growth. She still talked for hours but started to dress and act a little more appropriately. Eventually she moved from working in retail to working as a nursing assistant at a senior's centre. The lonely seniors loved her stories and loved listening to her. Encouraged by the staff at the senior's center, she got into nursing school and over the years helped a lot of people. She worked mostly with patients in a vegetative state at long term care facilities, spending hours talking to them as though they were still awake. This did not go unnoticed by their families, and she became one of the most popular nurses in the hospital where she worked.

She married an old flame having reconnected with Rick 3 years after she returned from Alaska. Both had grown up a lot and both were happy enough with themselves to finally be happy with each other. They bought a small hobby farm outside of town and keep pretty much to themselves and the members of their Star Trek group. Rick continues to work in the field of plumbing.

They even had kids, all of whom turned out to be beautiful and well-adjusted children. They find their parents to be weird but loving!

BJ
Numerous videos of him are available on the internet but nearly all have been debunked as videos of a sasquatch instead. He still bleeds after sex or urination and still looks back on his time with Beulla as the best weeks of his life! He was recently wounded in a vicious squirrel attack and continues to slowly recover, welcoming both thoughts <u>and</u> prayers.

Dennis
After Retail Depot Dennis returned to working as an electrician, this time in the employment of the city of Winnipeg police headquarters. He is still lazy and still eats too much but for the most part he goes about his duties and has managed to put three of the five children of the hotdog vendor in city hall through university. Surprisingly enough, he didn't die of a heart attack and continues to eat as though he were a family of seven.

Printed in Canada